Gallop to the Sea

SADDLE ISLAND SERIES #1

Gallop to the Sea

Sharon Siamon

Edited by Bobbie Chase
Proofread by Elizabeth McLean
Cover photos by Alexander Hafemann/iStockphoto (island)
    and Juniors Bildarchiv/Alamy (horse)
Cover and interior design by Jacqui Thomas

Printed and bound in Canada.

Library and Archives Canada Cataloguing in Publication
Siamon, Sharon
    Gallop to the sea/Sharon Siamon.

ISBN 1-55285-713-1
ISBN 978-1-55285-713-7

    1. Horses—Juvenile fiction. I. Title.

PS8587.I225G355 2006   jC813'.54   C2005-906778-0

The publisher acknowledges the support of the Canada Council and
the Cultural Services Branch of the Government of British Columbia
in making this publication possible. Whitecap Books also acknowledges
the financial support of the Government of Canada through the Book
Publishing Industry Development Program for our publishing activities.

Please note: Some places mentioned in this book are fictitious while
others are not.

The inside pages of this book are 100% recycled, processed chlorine-free
paper with 40% post-consumer content. For more information, visit
Markets Initiative's website: www.oldgrowthfree.com.

To Greg

Contents ◎

1

Race the Fog ☺

Jen Morrisey perched like a seabird on the highest point on Saddle Island. Her back was against the cliff called the Saddle Horn. Her feet swung into space.

Looking down made her dizzy.

Far, far below the sea came thundering in, throwing spray high into the air. From here, Jen could look out to sea or back to Dark Cove, the small village on the mainland where she lived.

She knew she shouldn't stay too long. Her shift at the riding stable, Harefield Farms, started in an hour.

Jen had been coming here for years, pretending it was all her island, her own special place, where she could be herself and not just Jen Morrisey, a kid from one of the poorest families in Dark Cove.

Seabirds circled, screaming, trying to scold her away from her perch on the Saddle Horn.

"This is my place," Jen screamed back. "My island!"

She knew Saddle Island really belonged to the Ridouts, even though old Maggie Ridout never came there.

Nobody comes, Jen thought fiercely. *Nobody but the birds and me.* Until now.

Jen scanned the shore with her binoculars, looking for the groove in the trees where the road ran down to the shore. The gossip was that today Maggie Ridout's nephew was coming back after almost twenty-five years and bringing his two kids. One was a boy Jen's age—twelve, and the other a girl, thirteen. Jen hoped it would be a short visit. She didn't want any trespassers on *her* island.

A white moving dot caught her attention. It was too small to be a car. Jen focused the binoculars and trained them on the moving dot again. It was a galloping white horse coming down the road into Dark Cove.

"Caspar!" Jen cried aloud. That darn horse was loose again—heading for the beach. She'd have to go and catch him or her boss, Hank Harefield, would have a fit.

She got to her feet, glanced out to the open sea, and the next second was scrambling back over the cliff top and down the corkscrew path through the trees.

That one glance had shown her a fog bank—a solid wall of white swooping toward the island.

Jen knew she had just minutes to head back for the mainland. The fog was a deadly white blanket that made it impossible to see where you were or where you were going.

Hurtling down through the forest, she grabbed at spruce boughs to slow her mad dash.

She burst out of the forest to bald gray rocks. A bright splash of red showed where her sea kayak was pulled up on the shore. Jen launched it into a sheltered channel, yanked on her spray skirt, stepped into the water and then the cockpit of the kayak. She reached for her paddle and shot out into the channel.

It would be a race. The fog was coming in fast. Jen's paddle flew. Left, right, left, right. She zoomed out of the channel between Saddle Island and its small neighbor, Teapot Island, which was just a bald bubble of rock. Keeping the islands on her left side, she paddled like fury for the beach at the head of Dark Cove.

Another quick glance over her shoulder showed she was losing the race. The fog had already closed around Saddle Island. In the next second she heard the first blast of the foghorn, a deep groaning sigh.

Moments later the fog swallowed her and the red kayak —white, bright, blinding fog.

Jen took a deep breath. She must keep on a straight line for the shore. Too far to the right and she'd hit the Grinder, a huge rock that jutted far out into the Cove, where many boats had been shattered in storms.

Left, right, left, right. The Grinder wasn't the worst danger. Jen knew she could get turned around and miss the shore completely. She could be lost for days and no one would find her.

Between the eerie groans of the foghorn, she paddled in a ghostly silence, her breath and the splash of the paddle the only sounds. Thank heavens for Caspar, she thought. If she hadn't seen the horse, she might have sat there on the cliff till the fog was on top of her.

How far was she from shore? Don't think, Jen told herself. Don't paddle too hard on the right or you'll go in circles.

Left, right, left, right.

She paddled until her arms ached, until her chest felt so tight she could hardly breathe.

Now she could hear the boom of waves crashing on the shore through the smothering fog. She drove on toward the sound, hoping she was aiming for the beach, not the rocks.

@@@

While Jen struggled to reach the shore, thirteen-year-old Kelsie MacKay was lost in the fog with her brother and father near Dark Cove.

Kelsie squirmed in the front seat of the rental car, trying to see through a blanket of white.

It had been a clear sunny day when their plane landed in Halifax. And then, when they were almost at the shore, they drove into a solid wall of fog.

"Not fair," Kelsie groaned to her father, Doug. "My first look at the ocean and I can't see a thing. It's just not fair!"

From the back seat came a groan. "At least you're in the front, and not squished by all these suitcases. Ouch! They're digging into me!"

Kelsie's brother, twelve-year-old Andy, had lost the toss for the front seat. But it didn't matter now, Kelsie thought bitterly. Nobody could see anything.

Including her dad! "I have no idea where we are ..." he muttered. "We must be getting close—we're going downhill."

The car slowed to a crawl.

"You mean we're lost?" Kelsie stared at her father's bearded profile. "I thought this was your hometown!"

"Sure." Her dad shrugged one shoulder. "Twenty-five years ago, when I was eighteen, it was home. Look for a blue house with brown trim. That'll be my aunt Maggie's."

"It's a little hard to see blue when everything's white, Dad."

"Roll down your window," he told her. "You might be able to see better."

Kelsie hit the button, the window descended, and a fine mist filled the car. It smelled fresh, like the forest. But there was a sharp tang to the air that was strange to Kelsie, who had lived her whole life in northern mining towns.

"Dad, what's that smell?" Andy called from the back seat.

"That, my son, is the smell of the sea."

The fresh sea air reminded her of riding through a forest of pines. Suddenly, Kelsie thought of Champ, the beautiful six-year-old palomino she'd left behind in the Yukon. Champ was golden like the sand along the Yukon River, golden like the far north summer light. He was on the other side of the country—a million miles away.

She would miss Champ so much! And in less than twenty-four hours, her dad would be gone, too. Off to his new job in a diamond mine.

Why did Dad have to take a job way off in the wilderness? Why did he have the bright idea of shipping her and Andy off to stay with an old aunt they'd never met?

What would this Aunt Maggie be like? Kelsie wondered. She strained to see through the fog, looking for a blue house. She could see the shapes of buildings, all different sizes, some high on the rocks, some hugging the road. Kelsie peered through the windshield, trying to pierce the fog that surrounded the car.

"Watch it, Dad!" she suddenly shouted. There was something standing in the middle of the road. A large white animal, almost invisible with the fog swirling around its shoulders.

Her dad stomped on the brakes, and blew the horn.

"Is it a moose?" Andy shouted. In the north, the worst kind of accident was hitting a moose. It could take the top off the car and your head with it.

"It's a white horse!" Kelsie reached for the door handle "Dad, let me out."

"Don't even think about it. Nobody's getting out." Her dad put the car back in gear. "Your Aunt Maggie is expecting us for dinner and we're already late. I'll drive around …"

"Wait!" Kelsie wrenched open the door and slid out into the fog. "We can't just leave a horse loose in the middle of the road!"

Ignoring her dad's shouts behind her, Kelsie ran to the horse's head. A frayed rope dangled from his halter. He stood like a white statue while she wound the rope around her hand to lead him off the road. Then, with a burst of power that lifted Kelsie off her feet, the big horse plunged into the roadside ditch and scrambled up the other side.

Her hand was tangled in the rope. She had no choice except to run with him, her feet flying over the wet grass.

"Whoa! Stop! Where are you taking me?" She prayed she wouldn't slip under the horse's hooves. *Never wrap a rope around your hand!* She could hear her riding instructor's warning in her head.

Too late! The rope burned and she was dragged up and down rocks, through backyards and gardens in the thick white fog. Then, just as suddenly, the horse jolted to a halt— so close to a building that his nose was almost pressed against the window.

The window flew open. A woman with long gray hair peered out. "Get that beast out of my garden, Jennifer Morrisey," she shouted. "He's trampling my flowers!"

Kelsie stepped forward, flooded with relief at finding herself in one piece. "Sorry."

"You're not Jen," the woman gasped. "Great heavens, girl, you … you could be the ghost of my sister Elizabeth!"

2

Horse in the Mist ◎

The gray-haired woman gaped at Kelsie as if she couldn't believe her eyes.

Kelsie unwound the rope from her hand and rubbed it to restore the circulation. "Come on, boy." She nudged the white horse. "Off the flowers."

She heard her dad's voice. "Kelsie? Where the blazes are you?"

"I'm here, Dad. Over by this blue house …"

"*Kelsie?*" The woman leaned farther out the window to peer at her. "Could you be my great-niece, Kelsie MacKay? What are you doing with that horse?"

"He was loose on the road. I was afraid he'd get hit." Kelsie stared back at the woman. Her hair was held back with two silver clips from a high forehead. Her nose was long and straight. Like Dad's. This crazy person must be his great-aunt Maggie. This blue house was his old home!

"Wretched horse always gets loose," the woman scolded. "He belongs up at Harefield Farms, but he seems to prefer it down here in Dark Cove."

Footsteps shuffled through the fog behind Kelsie.

"Douglas MacKay? Is that you?" the woman called through the swirling mist. "Come around to the door, for heaven's sake, and I'll let you in. I've been waiting dinner for half an hour."

"Sorry, Aunt Maggie," Kelsie's dad apologized.

"What'll I do with the horse?" Kelsie asked.

"Let him go," her aunt said firmly. "He'll find his way."

"But he might go back to the road. He might get hit. It's so foggy!"

"You're stubborn—just like my sister Elizabeth." Her aunt's sharp eyes looked Kelsie up and down. "But all right. Bring the horse to the side door. I'll meet you with a better rope and you can tie him to the apple tree."

ම ම ම

Meanwhile, with a harsh scraping jerk, Jen's kayak struck the shore. Reaching a hand through the foaming surf, she felt coarse sand. Gravel. Another wave lifted the kayak and tossed them farther ashore. She was beached. Safe.

Trembling, Jen wormed her way out of the kayak. She dragged it up the beach past the high tide mark and tied it to a driftwood log. Not secure in a storm, but good enough for now. Harefield would be furious, she was so late.

Sure enough, when she got to the Clam Shack where her mother worked, her mom handed her the phone as she ran into the kitchen. "Your boss wants to know where the heck you are," Chrissy Morrisey grunted, her eyes on the bubbling vat of hot grease and frying clams.

Harefield bellowed at Jen before she got the phone to her ear. "That crazy horse Caspar is gone again! See if you can find him and get him back here. And, in case it slipped your attention, YOU'RE LATE!"

"Sorry, Mr. Harefield. I got caught in the fog, out in my kayak."

Her mother threw her an angry look. She disapproved of Jen paddling alone. But right now, Jen was too tired and worried to care. How was she going to find a white horse in the fog?

@ @ @

Kelsie studied her Aunt Maggie bustling back and forth from the stove to the kitchen table. Her great-aunt's stern face was flushed with excitement and her gray eyes flashed.

She handed a plate of roast beef and potatoes to Kelsie's dad.

"You haven't changed, Douglas—except for that beard," she said in her low voice. "But the children! They don't look anything like they did in the pictures you sent."

Kelsie's dad looked guilty. Aunt Maggie always sent cards for their birthdays and at Christmas, but he hardly ever wrote back. Those pictures of us on the fridge must be three years old, Kelsie thought.

Aunt Maggie thrust a plate at Andy. "You look like your dad when he was your age—when he came to live with me.

Your hair stuck up in the front the same way. And you ..."
She paused with her hands on her hips and shook her head.
"Your grandmother, my big sister Elizabeth, had your green
eyes and pale skin and lovely auburn curls when she was thirteen. She was a wild girl, too, and stubborn as a stick."

Wild? Stubborn? Was that really what her grandmother
was like? Kelsie wondered. Dad never talked about his mom
and dad or how they died when he was thirteen.

Kelsie shifted uncomfortably in her chair.

"She was fidgety like you, too. Never sat still." Aunt Maggie
looked down her long nose at Kelsie. "I swear, seeing you
here, at this table, it's like Elizabeth is back in this kitchen ..."

Kelsie's dad interrupted. "Did you say something about
bumbleberry pie for dessert?"

Kelsie's throat closed as her dad and Andy gobbled huge
slices of rich dark pie. She'd been doing a lot of the cook-
ing for the three of them since her own mom died two years
before, and when she tried to bake a pie the crust had been
a soggy disaster.

"This is fantastic pie," her dad beamed. "Great crust."

"Dee–li–ci–ous!" Andy was stuffing his face.

Kelsie scraped back her chair. "I'm going out to check on
the horse."

"That animal will be fine," said Aunt Maggie firmly. "I
called Harefield Farms, and they'll come and pick him up.
Finish your pie."

"I'm full," Kelsie protested. "I just want to make sure he's
all right."

Aunt Maggie set her lips so that small lines creased around her mouth. "Stubborn," she muttered.

Kelsie's dad touched his aunt's lean arm. "Let Kelsie go out and see the horse. It was a long flight from the Yukon today."

"If you say so." The creases around Aunt Maggie's mouth hardened. "But she'll get wet through in this fog."

Kelsie took a deep breath as she escaped through the back door. Whew! She hoped her stay with Aunt Maggie would be short. Very short.

Once outside, she discovered Aunt Maggie had been right. The grass was drenched and her shoes were soon soaked. As she hurried to the apple tree, Kelsie breathed in the ocean smell again. Spicy, like a pine forest, but heavier. The damp air tasted salty when she licked her lips.

The white horse bobbed his big head when she came close and rubbed his forehead. "Glad to see you, too, buddy," she whispered. "Neither of us belong here, do we?"

Just then, she heard a voice. "Oh, great, you found Caspar!" A girl stepped out of the mist. She was wearing boots and a raincoat. Kelsie saw she was slender inside the bulky coat and about the same height as Andy. Strands of light brown hair escaped from her hood.

She stopped short, gazing at Kelsie. There was a pause, and then she spoke in a quick, breathless voice. "You must be Kelsie. I'm Jen. I've been looking everywhere for this guy."

"He was standing in the middle of the road." Kelsie stared at Jen's round face and blue eyes. "Is he your horse? My aunt said he belonged to a riding stable. Harefield Farms?"

"He does." Jen came forward to stroke Caspar's damp shoulder. "But I work there. And when Caspar gets loose and gallops down to the Cove, like he does *all* the time, I have to look for him."

"You know my name?" Kelsie asked.

"Sure I do." Jen shrugged. "You have a brother named Andy and you're Douglas MacKay's daughter. I live just over there …" She waved her hand vaguely to the right.

"You know my father, too?"

"Well, I don't know him, but I've heard about him, of course. He was born here, but he went away to work in the mines when he was young." Jen shrugged her slim shoulders again. "There's less than a hundred people in Dark Cove. Everybody knows everybody else's business. You'll get used to it."

"We're not going to be here that long," Kelsie said quickly. "We'll go back up north with my dad as soon as the mine has a house for us."

"Oh. I thought you were coming to live here." A smile turned up the corners of Jen's wide mouth.

"No." Kelsie stroked Caspar's nose. "Just to visit. But I'd love to ride while I'm here. What's Harefield Farms like?'

Jen's upturned smile turned down. "Not that great …"

She didn't finish. The sound of a vehicle rumbling up Aunt Maggie's lane interrupted her.

"That sounds like Hank Harefield's truck and trailer," gasped Jen.

Kelsie nodded. "My aunt called him."

"Oh! I wish she hadn't." Jen looked frightened. "I could have ridden Caspar back to the farm. Mr. Harefield's going to be steaming mad!"

Kelsie heard the porch door slam behind her. Aunt Maggie appeared, dressed in a yellow slicker and boots. She marched down the lane to meet the truck.

As it jarred to a stop, Kelsie could see the truck was pulling a small horse van. A short bald man with a red face squeezed himself out of the cab.

"Don't you dare drive that rig over my wet grass, Hank Harefield!" Aunt Maggie glowered down at the short man. "It'll leave great big muddy ruts."

"Calm down, woman, " Harefield sneered. "I'm not going to mess up your perfect property."

"See that you don't!" Aunt Maggie turned to Kelsie. "And you'd better come inside. You're drenched to the skin." She stomped away through the mist.

"I'm coming ..." Kelsie called after her, but she had no intention of obeying her aunt until she saw Caspar safely loaded. Harefield was wrenching open the trailer door.

"Jennifer! Get that flea-bitten excuse for a horse over here," he demanded, slapping his riding crop against his leg.

Jen threw a frightened glance at Kelsie as she fumbled to untie Caspar. "He hates loading," she whispered. "And he hates Harefield even worse. Can you help?"

"Sure ..." Kelsie had a sharp memory of Caspar lurching out of the ditch, dragging her with him. He was a powerful horse with a mind of his own. This could be dangerous!

Jen had Caspar's rope looped properly over her hand so it couldn't bind if he made a sudden move. "Come on, Caspar," she soothed. "It's just the trailer. It's not scary."

Caspar gave a loud whinny. His ears were pinned back and his tail clamped to his rear end. Harefield scuttled behind the truck as Jen led Caspar toward the trailer door. "Don't let that horse kick my trailer to pieces," he warned. "I'll shoot him if he does! He's long overdue for the glue factory, anyway."

Kelsie let down the ramp and positioned herself to the right of the trailer, blocking Caspar's escape route, but staying away from the sensitive zone of his head. Jen clucked and urged the big horse forward. As long as he could see Harefield he refused to set foot in the trailer, but once the man was out of sight he reluctantly edged up the ramp and into the small dark space.

"Good horse. Good Caspar!" Jen carefully lowered the butt bar and closed the trailer door. "He should be all right now," she called to Harefield. Moments later, the truck whined into gear and clattered away in the mist.

"Thanks," Jen turned to Kelsie. "You're great with horses."

Kelsie glared at the disappearing trailer. "What an idiot. Imagine threatening to kill Caspar. I guess I won't be riding at his stable!"

Jen sighed. "It's the only place around here to ride." She looked up at Kelsie. "I hope you come out to the Farm, even if you're only going to be here a little while. Caspar obviously likes you." Her blue eyes lit up. "And wait till you ride along the shore—it's the best feeling in the world!"

"I can't wait to see the ocean." Kelsie waved at the fog that surrounded them. "I feel like I'm in a movie with the lights turned off."

Jen smiled at her. "You'll see. It's like magic when the sun comes out."

Just then Kelsie heard her father calling from the blue house. "Kel? Are you still out here? Your aunt wants you inside."

"All right." Kelsie waved goodbye to Jen. Did she have to do everything her aunt said? she wondered as she sprinted to the back door. For how long?

3

Bad News! ⊚

Jen hurried home through the fog. Her house was smaller than Maggie Ridout's and stood alone on a smooth dome of rock, looking out at the sea.

Jen thought about Kelsie as she ran. "I didn't think I'd like that girl, but I do," she said to herself. She liked the way Kelsie's green eyes sparkled when she talked, and the calm way she pitched in to help load Caspar.

"And if the MacKays are leaving soon," Jen carried on her conversation with herself, "I guess I don't have to worry that they're going to take over Saddle Island. Maybe Kelsie won't even hear about it."

⊚⊚⊚

But at that moment Kelsie was staring at a framed map of Saddle Island. "Dad!" she called. "Come and look at this—it looks like the map of a treasure island, or something."

Andy came pelting across the hall from his bedroom. "Treasure map? Let me see that!"

The map hung over one of the iron beds in Kelsie's tiny upstairs room. Like Andy's room across the hall, it had wide planked floors and slanted walls with a bed on either side and a small window at the end. There were patchwork quilts on the beds and faded mats on the floor.

Doug MacKay stooped through the low doorway and bent over to peer at the map. He unhooked it and sat on the bed with it propped in his lap. Kelsie sat close on one side and Andy on the other.

"This is a map of Saddle Island," their father told them. "There are lots of stories about pirates, shipwrecks and smugglers leaving treasure there, but no one in our family has found anything in over a hundred years."

"You mean it's our island?" Andy's brown eyes were huge.

"It's your Aunt Maggie's island," his father corrected him. "Part of the Ridout farm. Your great-great-grandfather pioneered the whole thing with horses."

"Horses—on an island—and our family owns it." Kelsie stroked the faded map with her finger. "It sounds exciting! Can you take us out there, Dad?"

Her father stood up abruptly and hung the map back on the wall.

"I don't think your Aunt Maggie would want us going out there."

"Why …?" Kelsie started to say, but her dad went on.

"Anyhow, I have to leave tomorrow afternoon and there's a lot of stuff to get first." He counted the items off on his fingers. "Bikes for each of you so you can get around. A motor for my old dory, if it's still in the fish house, so Andy can go fishing. Riding lessons for you, Kelsie …"

Andy looked down at the floor and scuffed his feet on the mat. "I wish you didn't have to go so soon."

"So do I, but I have to start my new job." Doug scrubbed Andy's short hair gently. "Hey! Be careful with that mat—it's a family heirloom."

"This old rug?" Andy looked up, surprised.

"Hooked by your great-grandmother, the wife of Roland Ridout. He was a wild man—some say a smuggler, a rum-runner in his time."

Andy's face cleared. "Really?"

"Yup, I'll tell you all about him some day. Right now, we'd better get to bed. Aunt Maggie's orders!"

ⓠⓠⓠ

Meanwhile, Jen popped popcorn in the microwave and took it into the living room to share with her mom.

"I met the MacKay girl today," Jen told her mother. "The one from out west. She helped me catch Caspar."

"Maggie Ridout's great-niece? What's she like?" Jen's mother reached for a handful of popcorn. Chrissy was a slight woman, with silky brown hair like Jen's.

Jen collapsed on the couch, the bowl in her lap. "Nice," she said briefly. "Pretty. And she's good with horses."

"Then she must be just about perfect," Chrissy teased. "Did you see her father, Doug MacKay?"

"Nope. He didn't come out." Jen shook her head. "Kelsie

has all this curly dark red hair, and she's tall and looks like she's not afraid of anything or anyone."

"That's interesting," Jen's mother said slowly. "That's exactly how I remember Doug MacKay's mother, Elizabeth Ridout. I was just a little girl when she died, but I've never forgotten what she looked like—so lovely and proud. I always wondered what happened to Doug—losing his parents so early."

"Well, I didn't see him," Jen said again, "or Kelsie's brother, Andy."

"Andy's about your age, isn't he?" Jen's mother munched popcorn. "Might be a boyfriend for you, Jen. A romantic lad from far away."

"Don't tease, Mom!" Jen groaned. But she couldn't help wondering whether Andy MacKay would be as interesting as his sister.

☙ ☙ ☙

Kelsie had trouble falling asleep that first night in Dark Cove. The slanted ceilings pressed down on her and the image of Harefield brandishing his riding crop haunted her. What an awful man!

In the next room, she heard Andy turn restlessly in his bed. She worried about how he was going to feel when Dad left tomorrow.

She must have dozed off, because it was pitch dark when voices from the kitchen woke her.

"I hope that boy won't spend all his time in the boat.

There will be chores for him to do around the house."

It was Aunt Maggie's voice carrying clearly up the stairs!

"Don't scold, Aunt," Kelsie heard her dad say. He sounded tired.

Kelsie lay stiff and flat under the patchwork quilt, trying not to shiver. How would she stand it—even for a short time? She heard her aunt's voice again.

"I have to tell you the truth, Douglas. The money's welcome. But it seems a crazy idea to send two children to live with an old woman."

"You're not old!"

"Fifty-five. Not young."

"Kelsie's a teenager. You took me in when I was her age and I turned out all right."

"That was different. You came from Dark Cove, and you knew me, and this house."

Kelsie heard her father sigh. "I can't take them with me, Aunt Maggie. But I can make a lot of money at this new diamond mine—they're paying top wages. I can save enough to send both kids to college … and help you out."

"I know all that." Kelsie heard the sound of a chair being shoved back from the table and water running. "Well, we'll have to try. But I'll take no nonsense from those two. I'll look after them in my own way."

"Be kind to Andy. He needs some mothering."

"Andy will be fine. It's your girl. She's got her grandmother Elizabeth's wild spirit. I can see it in her. She's impulsive—acts without thinking. I'll have to use a firm hand, or …"

"Kelsie's a good girl. She's bursting with energy and she's smart and has strong feelings for the things she loves."

"So did your mother, Elizabeth, and look what happened to her!"

"I don't like you talking about Kelsie that way. She's her own person. I don't want her growing up in a rough mining camp—it's no place for a thirteen-year-old girl."

There was a long pause.

"They've had a tough time with their mother passing away. The way I see it, it would do them both good to stay in one place for a few years."

A few years! Kelsie gripped the edge of the quilt between cold fingers. She hadn't realized that Dad was even thinking of leaving them with Aunt Maggie for more than a month or two!

@@@

The next day, Sunday, was dark and rainy. The fog bank hung over the ocean like a curtain. It felt like the cold wind blew the dampness right into your bones, Kelsie thought.

She waited for a chance to talk to her father about the conversation she'd overheard the night before. It couldn't be true that he was leaving them in Dark Cove for *years*!

But her dad was busy, tuning up the motor he'd found in the back of the Dark Cove Garage when he went to buy two used bikes. He and Andy fussed over the motor and his old green dory while Kelsie hung around the dock and watched the dark water in front of Aunt Maggie's rise with the tide.

One of the last things her dad did was phone Harefield Farms about riding lessons for her. "You can bike up there tomorrow," he told Kelsie. "Aunt Maggie says it isn't far."

"Dad!" Kelsie finally exploded. "How long will we have to stay here? Tell me the truth!"

"We've talked about this." Her dad paused with the phone still in his hand. "At least until the mining company builds housing for families."

"Well, it'd better not be too long." Kelsie threw back her head and glared at him. "Aunt Maggie doesn't like me."

"Listen, Kel." Her father stroked her unruly curls. "Maggie's strict, but she's kind. She raised me from the time I was thirteen, so I should know. I'm sending her money every month to pay for your board, and she needs that money to keep the house. Follow her rules and you'll find her fair."

So that's it, Kelsie sighed to herself. Aunt Maggie is taking us because she needs the cash. She's fair if you follow her rules—you could say the same thing about a school principal or a prison warden!

Finally it was time for Doug to climb into the rental car and head for the airport and his flight to Whitehorse, in the Yukon.

Time for final hugs in the rain.

"You'll be three thousand miles away." Andy's whisper was hoarse. "What if we need you?"

"You'll call me, and I'll come."

"Promise?"

"Of course."

But he hadn't said the word promise, Kelsie noticed.

When their dad's car disappeared down the lane, Andy took to his boat, circling the dock like a gull with a wounded wing. Kelsie wondered if she should tell her brother what she'd overheard the night before. No, she decided. Wait to see how things turned out.

If only this rain would stop!

4

Wild Ride ⊚

Kelsie woke up Monday morning and groaned, remembering where she was. She rolled over. Sunlight was blasting through the window, spreading across the faded rug.

Kelsie jumped out of bed, threw open the small window and stuck her head out.

"Jen was right!" she cried. "It's like magic."

The fog and rain had rolled away.

She could see the ocean at last.

The whole of Dark Cove was spread out in front of her, sparkling in the morning sun. Kelsie had lived near lakes, large and small, but she had never seen anything like this water. The ocean was deep, dark blue, the most dazzling blue Kelsie could imagine.

The cove was dotted with islands, but in one place, near the center, you could see past the islands and look way out to the edge of the sky. There was nothing out there but blue water, all the way to the coast of Africa, Dad had told her.

Down below, she could see Aunt Maggie, bent over a small vegetable patch. Kelsie glanced at her watch—only six-thirty—and already Aunt Maggie was gardening. She must like to get up early, too.

She slipped into her jeans and T-shirt and ran lightly down the stairs, trying not to wake Andy. He'd slow her down.

Outside, she walked quickly past her aunt, who was on her knees among the cabbages with her back to Kelsie. She had a feeling she should stop and say good morning, but the pull of the ocean was stronger, and once safely past, she raced down the path to the dock.

The waves rolled in under its dark timbers and each one was full of sunlight and waving seaweed. Out there, beyond the islands, the waves were flecked with white foam. To the left was a narrow strip of beach that stretched along one whole side of the cove. There, the waves rolled in with a soft "boom" followed by a long sigh.

Wait—Kelsie scanned the shore harder. There was a horse running along the strip of beach. A white horse!

Kelsie ran back up the dock and found the path that led along the shore, past other docks and fish shacks, and small houses, each nestled perfectly in the curve of the rocks. She saw all this without looking. Her eyes were fixed on the horse and rider, who had almost reached her end of the beach.

It was Jen, riding bareback on Caspar.

"Jen!" she shouted, running faster.

Jen rode him up the rocky shingle. "Whoa!" She stopped Caspar in front of Kelsie. "He got away again, last night," she puffed in her breathless voice. "Galloped right to the sea, like he always does. I have to get him back in time for the first riding class at seven-thirty or Mr. Harefield will have a fit."

She grinned down at Kelsie. "But this time I'll ride him up to Harefield Farms. No more scary trailer rides for this guy!"

Kelsie couldn't take her eyes off Caspar. In full sunlight he glowed. He was sturdily built but a bit swaybacked. Jen fitted comfortably behind his withers, with her hands buried in his mane.

"Could I ride him?" Kelsie had never ridden bareback, but it looked amazing. There was the ocean, and the damp sand with Caspar's hoofprints along the edge of the water.

Jen took a quick look at her watch. "I guess so—I still have a few minutes." She turned Caspar around on the path. "Let's go back down to the sand and you can get up on that rock to mount him." She pointed to a large flat rock.

Kelsie ran after them, slipping and sliding down the gravel bank to the beach. She climbed the flat rock and threw her leg over Caspar's broad back while Jen held him firmly by the mane.

"Now grip his mane here, and here," Jen said. "Ride him down the beach and back, but don't let him go in the water. He loves swimming."

She let go of his mane.

Caspar knew immediately that he had someone on his back who had never ridden without a saddle, let alone along an ocean shore. He plunged straight into the waves, and nothing Kelsie could do, from shouting to pummeling his sides with her heels, could make him stop.

The water was icy cold.

Spray dashed up as they splashed through the shallow surf. Kelsie gasped as waves sloshed over them. Would Caspar keep swimming straight out to sea?

But once outside the surf, Caspar swam in a large circle, heading back to shore. Kelsie's feet and legs were numb with cold, but she was laughing with the pure joy of riding a swimming horse in the ocean.

It was a fantastic feeling!

Jen was waiting anxiously when he stomped up on the shore, water cascading off his white hide.

"Now we'll be really, really late," she gasped. "But it was almost worth it, watching you …" She burst into giggles as Kelsie slid from Caspar's back. "You looked so surprised."

"Sorry," Kelsie apologized. "I couldn't turn him." She gave Caspar an affectionate pat. "I think you like to get your own way, don't you? Independent, like me."

"I've got to go." Jen climbed on Caspar's back again. "Try to come out to Harefield Farms later. I'll be there all day," she called over her shoulder as she galloped away.

@ @ @

Kelsie watched the big horse canter down the beach with Jen on his back. She shivered with cold and excitement. What would Aunt Maggie say when she turned up dripping wet for breakfast?

The sun was shining on the black rocks at the end of the beach. Maybe if she sat there in the wind she'd dry off enough to dash upstairs for dry clothes. Worth a try.

The biggest of the rocks was shaped like the prow of a ship. Kelsie climbed over the slimy seaweed around its base to perch on the pointed end, with her bare feet hanging.

She sat for a long time soaking up the morning sun, watching the light dance on the waves.

A fishing boat was coming into the Cove. It was turquoise and white, and on its deck Kelsie could see a young man. The sun shone on his dark hair and strong features. He was bending over a net, but he suddenly looked up and saw her and waved with both arms.

Kelsie waved back and then felt her face flush. She didn't even know the guy and he was waving at her like a wild man. What was the matter with him?

She looked down into the crystal clear water of the cove, confused. A few minutes later a glance showed her the fishing boat was gone.

With a sigh, Kelsie flopped on her stomach and studied the strange world of the ocean bottom. Below the rock were tiny rock pools, carved by the waves. In deeper pools, yellowy-green seaweed swayed and danced, catching the light. Tiny fish, so small that at first you couldn't see them, darted in and out among the strands of seaweed.

You have to sit very still and concentrate to see into this magical world, she thought. For instance, those sea snails looked stuck to the rocks just under the water. But if you watched long enough you saw them move, passing each other at a snail's pace.

She stared into the water for a long time, letting the sun warm her back.

Suddenly she heard a loud bellow from behind. "Stay where you are!"

Kelsie jerked her head around, almost losing her balance and slipping into the sea.

The beach behind her had disappeared under water.

And there, across a stretch of foaming surf, was the good-looking young guy she'd seen on the fishing boat!

5

The Grinder ◎

"You shouldn't be up there," the young man shouted. "It's dangerous!"

The large rock Kelsie was sitting on was now an island, with great gushes of water roaring between it and the shore each time a wave boomed in.

Kelsie gasped. Where had the beach gone? Where had all that water come from? She started sliding down the rock.

"Wait! Don't move. Let me help you." He waded into the foaming surf, leaping from rock to rock, balanced like a tight-rope walker between the shore and the big rock. He reached out a lean, strong arm. "When I give the word, jump!" he yelled. "Don't be afraid, I'll catch you."

Kelsie stared at him. He'd catch her? Her heart pounded.

"Now!" he shouted.

Kelsie took a deep breath and jumped. The young man caught her with one arm, swung her toward the shore and then jumped himself. He let her down on the coarse grass and stood looking down at her.

"You shouldn't be out on the Grinder at high tide," he said, puffing with exertion. "We lose a few tourists every year along this coast just like that."

"The Grinder? That's what you call that rock?" Kelsie tried to pretend she hadn't just been swooped up and rescued. Waves were now sweeping over the Grinder, each one throwing up a plume of spray. She looked up at the young man. "Where's your boat?"

"At the dock." He pointed down the beach. "I couldn't bring her any closer—a lot of ships have been wrecked on that rock."

He shook his dark head. "I thought I'd better come over and see if you were still here. There's a bad undertow between the Grinder and the shore when the tide comes in. It's dangerous just trying to get off."

Kelsie got to her feet. She was suddenly very aware that her hair was a tangled mess, her clothes were damp and stuck to her body at odd places, and she probably looked like something that had been towed by a four-wheeler. And this guy must think she was a total idiot, waving to him when he was trying to warn her!

"Th—thanks for helping me," she stammered, anxious to get away.

The young man grinned, a devastating one-sided grin. "You might not be thanking me in a minute," he said. "I called your Aunt Maggie from our dock, and here she comes. … Sorry."

"How do you know who …?" Kelsie had no time to finish.

Her aunt came flying along the shore path toward them in her baggy sweater and pants. Seconds later, she was on them like a whirlwind, her face flushed from running and fury.

"What on earth were you doing on the Grinder with the tide coming in?" she gasped. "Don't you know people drown doing stupid things like that?"

Kelsie shook her head. "The rock was connected to the beach when I climbed up here," she told her aunt. "I've heard about the tide, but I didn't think it came in so fast."

"Well, now you know." Aunt Maggie gave her a hard look. "Thank you, Gabriel. I'll take it from here."

Kelsie felt like a little kid as Aunt Maggie gripped her hand and led her back along the path, still scolding at the top of her lungs. Gabriel—that was his name. What must he think!

"Imagine how I felt when I called you and Andy for breakfast and you weren't upstairs." Aunt Maggie swung her around to face her. "And then the phone rings ..." She choked, staring at Kelsie. "Why are your clothes all wet? Don't *tell* me you've been in the ocean?"

"I met Jen, and Caspar," Kelsie admitted. "I was only supposed to ride him along the beach, but he had other ideas."

Aunt Maggie threw up her hands. "Swimming? On a horse?" Her voice rose. "The first day your father's not here and already ..." Her voice broke off and she looked out to sea.

Kelsie shifted from one foot to the other. She was afraid Aunt Maggie might start to cry, but her aunt shook back her long gray hair and straightened her shoulders.

"It's a good thing Caspar's a big strong horse," she sniffed, "because there's a wicked undertow, like I said." She stared at Kelsie, shaking her head. "I swear, girl, you're going to give me nothing but misery. There are going to be some new rules around here! "

Kelsie followed her meekly back to the blue house. How had she gotten into so much trouble so fast?

@ @ @

Aunt Maggie laid out her list of new rules at breakfast.

Andy and Kelsie sat at the kitchen table while she served them enormous blueberry pancakes swimming in Nova Scotia maple syrup. The hot blueberries burst in your mouth, but Kelsie was too miserable to taste them with her aunt waving her spatula in her face.

"First, I expect you to show up for meals—on time. And that includes breakfast." She glared at Kelsie.

"Second, there will be absolutely NO swimming off the beach. There's an undertow that can sweep you off your feet and suck you under before you can yell for help. Are you listening to me, Andy?"

Andy gulped down his bite of pancake. "Yes, Aunt Maggie. Yum. These are the best pancakes I ever ate."

Traitor, Kelsie thought. *After all the pancakes I've made for you …*

"And third," her aunt went on, pointing her spatula at Andy, "you're to stay right in front of this house with your boat—I don't want you out of my sight until I see that you respect the ocean. Do you understand?"

"Aunt Maggie," Kelsie broke in, "we want to go out to Saddle Island."

Her aunt's face grew pale. She seemed to shrink into her baggy sweater. "You are not, do you hear me, *not* to go near Saddle Island," she said in a hoarse voice. "So many boats have been wrecked on that island—"

"But Aunt Maggie," Kelsie tried again. "Andy's been driving motorboats since he was six. Every place we've lived there's been a lake …"

"The ocean is *not* a lake!" Aunt Maggie's pale face flushed with anger. "That's what I'm trying to tell you. There are tides and fog and sudden storms." She took a deep breath and looked each of them in the eye in turn. "Those are my rules, and I expect you to obey them. Now that your father's gone, I'm in charge."

"Aunt Maggie," Andy suddenly cried. "Your pancakes!"

Smoke was rising from the stove and the kitchen filled with a burning smell.

"Now look what you've made me do!" Aunt Maggie grabbed the pan off the stove and waved her arms. "Clear out of my kitchen, both of you."

@ @ @

Andy and Kelsie escaped out into the sunshine. Kelsie followed her brother down to the dock.

"I'm *totally* disgusted with you," she told him. "You sold out for a stack of pancakes."

"I don't know what you're talking about." Andy went into

the small fish house at the top of the dock to get his rod and reel. He came out and shut the door of the old cedar-shingled building.

"I'm talking about caving in to Aunt Maggie's rules without a fight." Kelsie followed him down the dock. "I thought you wanted to go out to Saddle Island. You can't do that if you have to stay in sight of the house."

She looked over her shoulder at the blue house sitting smugly in the sun. Its two windows on either side of the door looked like eyes, staring out at the bay.

Andy shrugged. "Dad told us there's no treasure on Saddle Island anymore," he muttered. He headed for his green dory with his fishing rod over his shoulder. It was low tide, and a ramp at the end of the dock slanted steeply down to a floating platform where his boat was tied.

"I can fish right here and catch lots of stuff." He hopped into the boat with Kelsie following hard on his heels. "Look, I caught these crabs already." He showed her two pink crabs in the bottom of a bucket.

"I still say you're giving in too easily." Kelsie plopped down on the floating platform, which rose and fell with the waves. "Don't you want to go out there?" She waved her hand at the Cove and its dark green islands. "Don't you want to explore everything?"

Andy looked down, fiddling with his fishing rod. "Sure, but we have to try to get along with Aunt Maggie."

"Maybe *you* do! I'm not listening to a crazy old lady who thinks we're going to fall in the ocean and drown any minute!" Kelsie announced. Her humiliation in front of Gabriel still stung. "I'm glad I don't have to stay here and put up with her all day. I'm going to Harefield Farms for my riding lesson, and if she asks, say I'm staying for lunch!"

6

Harefield Farms ◎

Kelsie pedaled up the steep hill out of Dark Cove. It was a long climb and her bike was old. She stopped at the top to rest and look back at the breathtaking scene below.

From up here it looked as if a giant had flung a handful of houses at the shore of the Cove. Some were so close they looked as if they were in each other's backyards. Others, like Aunt Maggie's, were far apart. Kelsie could see the dock and the fish house and the old barn behind the blue house. There were apple trees and a hay meadow. It had been a real farm, she thought, in the past.

She could also see the three islands that had been part of the farm—a long skinny one near the shore, a short fat one with almost no trees, and then ..."That's Saddle Island," she breathed in excitement. "It must be!" The largest of the three islands had a high cliff at each end and a low section, like the seat of a saddle, in the middle.

"Why did Aunt Maggie get so upset when we said we were going there?" Kelsie asked herself, "So upset she let the pancakes burn." There was a secret about the island—something that made her angry, and sad.

From up here on the ridge above Dark Cove, the islands looked like stepping stones, they were so close to each other. It was maddening, being forbidden to explore them.

"I'll get there," Kelsie vowed. "I'll figure out a way."

But first, there was Harefield Farms.

ල ල ල

As she biked into the stable yard, Kelsie saw no sign of Caspar or Jen. Harefield Farms consisted of a low barn surrounded by corrals and riding rings. There were a few horses in each of the corrals and in one ring some little girls on ponies having a lesson.

A short, bald man was smacking a brown horse with a riding crop, trying to get him to go through a gate. Harefield! Kelsie recognized him as the man who'd come to collect Caspar two nights ago.

She jumped off her bike. "That's no way to treat a horse!" The shout rose to her throat before she could stop it. She gulped it back as the brown horse finally skittered through the gate, ears back and tail clamped in fear.

Kelsie glared at Harefield as he strutted toward her.

"Here for your lesson?" He gave her a greasy smile.

She nodded, still so angry she couldn't speak.

"Well, go and see Jen in the barn. She'll show you around. Then you can choose a horse and tack up. Let me know when you're ready."

"Y … you?" Kelsie stammered. "You're my *riding instructor?*"

"At the moment." Harefield stroked his shiny bald head. "We're a bit short-staffed. I've only got Marci." He pointed to the woman conducting the pony class. "And she's just for beginners."

Kelsie gulped. "I'll go and see Jen." She wheeled her bike to the barn and leaned it against the wall, then dragged open the door and fled inside.

"Jen!" she called as she ran down the center aisle.

A whinny came from a stall near the far end, where wide doors were open to a sunny field. A large white head poked out over the top of the stall.

Caspar. And he looked fine.

"Jen?" Kelsie called again.

"I'm here."

Kelsie found her sitting on a bale of hay in an alcove opposite Caspar's stall. Her light brown hair hung over her face.

"What's wrong?"

Jen looked up. She'd been crying!

"Harefield was really mad when Caspar showed up late and wet," Jen sniffed. "One more strike and he's out, that's what Harefield said."

"What does that mean? Would he sell Caspar?"

"Worse. He'd send Caspar to auction," Jen moaned. "Horses that go to the auction almost never get good homes. Sometimes they even get slaughtered for meat, or fertilizer."

"That's horrible!" Kelsie strode over to pat Caspar's velvety nose. "This is my fault," she groaned. "He wouldn't be wet or late if it weren't for our ride in the sea."

"That's not the only thing he's done," Jen said sadly.

"What else?" Kelsie turned to look at her stricken face.

"Well," sighed Jen, "we had a summer festival here in June, and Harefield hitched Caspar to a hay wagon to drive in the parade. Harefield and Miss Summerfest rode on the wagon."

"What happened?" Kelsie stroked Caspar's powerful white neck, picturing him in harness.

"Caspar wrecked the parade," Jen said sorrowfully. "He ran straight for the water like he did this morning, and Miss Summerfest ended up in the Cove. Her dress was *ruined*, and Harefield's top hat fell in the water. Everybody laughed at him."

"Good. He's such a pompous stuffed shirt."

Jen went on, "And a week later Caspar stepped on Harefield's foot while he was saddling him. He didn't mean to, but Harefield had to go around on crutches for a week. He thinks Caspar does these things on purpose—that he's out to get him."

"Oooh …" Kelsie gave Caspar a rub between his ears, trying not to grin. "And now you turn up soaking wet. I guess you're not what you'd call the ideal school horse, are you?"

"He's wonderful!" Jen cried. "You can put the littlest kid on Caspar's back and he'll be so gentle. He's just too big and strong for Harefield to bully."

"He *is* a bully!" Kelsie blazed. "I saw him beating on a brown horse as I rode up."

"That'll be Zeke. He's scared of Harefield, that's why he's balky sometimes. He goes great for me."

"How can you stand to work for that man?" Kelsie asked indignantly.

"I work for him because I need the money and I love the horses," Jen told her. She stood up and grabbed a broom. "Quiet—here he comes!" Head down, she swept furiously at the barn floor.

Harefield stalked toward them.

He nodded to Kelsie. "I see you found your friend. Glad to see you hard at work, Jennifer. Don't waste too much time on that horse." He motioned to Caspar's stall. "He's not worth the trouble."

He turned back to Kelsie. "Are you ready to choose a horse to ride? Your father arranged for lessons twice a week for you."

"Could I ride Caspar?" Kelsie tried to make the question sound innocent, but Harefield shook his head violently.

"Not on your life! I'm keeping Caspar shut in his stall. Then maybe he'll learn not to jump fences or break gates!"

"In that case I'll just check out the rest of the horses and look around today," Kelsie said. "Is it okay if I help Jen while I'm here? I like working in barns."

Harefield looked at her suspiciously. "I guess so. As long as the work gets done."

"Can we let Caspar out in the corral while we clean his stall?" Jen asked.

"No!" Harefield planted his legs like a stubborn horse. "Keep him locked up in here for the rest of the day."

Caspar turned slowly in his box stall until he showed Harefield his rump. Then he lifted his tail and let out a stream of manure.

Kelsie stifled a giggle. That horse knew how to insult Harefield, but good!

"Don't laugh," Jen whispered to Kelsie as Harefield strode angrily away. "We have to keep Caspar out of trouble, and I need this job."

"Don't worry. I'll come out every day while I'm here and help you," Kelsie promised.

7

Gabriel ꧁

"I don't know what I'm going to do about all the lessons Dad paid for," Kelsie sighed as she and Jen rode away from Harefield Farms on their bikes late that afternoon. "I'm sure not taking any from *him*."

"He doesn't know much, that's for sure," agreed Jen. "It was his wife, Lenore, who set up the stable. Caspar was her horse."

"What happened to Lenore?" Kelsie asked as they turned onto the main road that led down to the Cove.

"She ran off with a fitness instructor from Halifax."

"Oooh. That explains why Harefield hates Caspar so much. I wish I could buy him … maybe I could!"

"It must be nice to have the money to buy whatever you want," sighed Jen.

Kelsie glanced over at her. Jen's bike was even older and more decrepit than her secondhand one. "We're not rich," she said quickly. "I think Dad was feeling guilty because he had to leave us, so he bought us stuff—like this bike and riding lessons."

"But he makes big money in the mines, doesn't he?" Jen asked shyly.

"Oh. Sure. But all the jobs are way up north, and we're always moving." Kelsie said. "Since I was born I've lived in South Porcupine, Flin Flon, Uranium City, Fort MacPherson and Whitehorse—five different towns."

"That sounds exciting," Jen sighed. "I've never been anywhere."

"Tell me about your family," said Kelsie. "You know all about mine."

Jen pedaled faster. "There's just me and Mom. My dad left when I was a baby. Mom doesn't make much, working at the Clam Shack, which is why I need to work at Harefield Farms. Otherwise, I'd never get to ride."

Kelsie struggled to keep up. No wonder Jen seemed older than twelve—she had a lot of responsibility.

They had reached the crest of the hill above the Cove. "Slow down!" Kelsie called to Jen. "I don't think my brakes are good enough to go downhill this fast!"

She squeezed the hand brakes. They were horribly mushy. Her hands went all the way to the end without much happening.

The hill ahead was steep.

"You go ahead!" she called to Jen. "Come over tonight and you can meet my brother Andy."

"All right!" Jen was already zooming away around a curve in the road.

Kelsie knew she should get off the bike and walk. Riding it down this hill was like riding a runaway horse! But she hated to give in. "Come on!" she shouted as the bike sped up. "Work, you stupid brakes."

She squeezed so hard her hands ached. But the brakes didn't respond and the bike picked up speed.

They flew around the curve.

Kelsie had a vision of her Aunt Maggie's face if she came home bruised and bloody… she might forbid her to go to Harefield Farms. With a cry of regret, Kelsie turned the wheel toward a grassy ditch at the side of the road. At least it would be a soft landing.

The bike hit the ditch at an angle, throwing Kelsie into the air.

"Ooof!" she landed on her back, the breath knocked out of her.

The next second, a truck came up the road. Kelsie rolled over, took one look at the driver, and buried her face in the dirt. He mustn't see her. He mustn't stop!

It was the young man from the boat. Gabriel.

☙ ☙ ☙

"I'm fine, I'm fine!" Kelsie cried, as Gabriel tried to lift her up. "I don't need help!"

"Glad to hear it. So why are you lying in a ditch face down?"

"I was resting." Kelsie shook off his hand. She couldn't admit she was hiding from him!

"I see." Gabriel's lopsided grin stayed on his face as he dragged her bike out of the ditch and set it on the road. "Looks like your bike might need some fixing up."

"It needs better brakes, that's for sure," Kelsie muttered. "I just hit the ditch to slow down. I did it on purpose." She shoved back her tangled curls and waved her hand. "So, you can go on—wherever it was you were going."

"Sure you don't want a ride back to your Aunt Maggie's?"

"NO!"

"No." The grin stayed put. "Might not be a good idea showing up with me—twice in one day." He reached out a hand to help her out of the ditch. "I can see things are going to be a lot more interesting in Dark Cove with you MacKay kids here."

Kids! He was laughing at her. Kelsie accepted the warm strong grip of Gabriel's hand to scramble out of the ditch and then snatched her hand away. "Thank you," she said formally. "I'm glad you're so amused."

The grin faded. "Didn't mean to hurt your feelings. Just teasing. Are you sure you're all right?"

Kelsie looked away from his serious dark eyes. "Fine. Really." She picked up her bike and walked away down the hill. He thought she was a kid!

8

In the Barn @

Jen paddled her red kayak over to Aunt Maggie's floating dock after dinner.

"I call my boat *Seahorse*," she told Kelsie, who had come to help her tie up. "It washed up on the beach after a hurricane a couple of years ago. No one claimed it so I fixed it up and bought a paddle."

Kelsie ran her hand down *Seahorse*'s shiny side. "Is it hard to learn to kayak?"

"Easier than riding a real horse." Jen grinned, wriggling out of the cockpit.

The two sat on the Ridout dock swinging their feet.

"I keep thinking about poor Caspar," Kelsie grieved. "It broke my heart to leave him— "

Just then, Andy came down the dock with a bucket in his hand. He stopped, staring at Jen.

"This is my brother Andy," Kelsie introduced him.

"Hi." Jen and Andy said together.

Andy looked away, pretending Jen wasn't there. He didn't

say anything to her or even glance in her direction. Instead he untied his boat and scrambled aboard.

He yanked on the starter cord. An explosion of noise and a cloud of black smoke shattered the quiet of Dark Cove. Andy zoomed around in circles, the prow of the dory high in the air.

Kelsie and Jen waved the fumes away. "Sorry about that," Kelsie apologized. "My dad says Andy will shake the old boat to pieces, running that motor so fast!"

"It's all right." Jen smiled her upturned smile. "I don't mind motorboats. When I was a little kid there were boats in this cove all the time—little dories and great big fishing boats."

She looked wistfully at Andy, who was showing off by standing in the back of the boat while he steered in circles. "I think your brother's kind of cute. How old is he?"

"Twelve. But he acts like a five-year-old most of the time. You're twelve, and you're twice as mature." Kelsie stared at Jen. "Do you really think he's cute?"

Jen tore her eyes away from Andy and the boat. "Yeah." She looked embarrassed.

Kelsie shrugged. "Well, he's working hard to impress you, so maybe he thinks you're cute, too."

She looked around the cove. "What happened to all the boats?"

"The fish plant closed." Jen pointed to a dilapidated building to the right of the Ridout dock. "Everybody used to work there. Your Aunt Maggie, too."

The big gray building had boards over the windows and grass growing up around the steps. In front of it was a long cement pier.

"Whose boat is that?" Kelsie pointed to a large cabin cruiser tied up to the pier.

"That's Harefield's floating palace, the *Lord Selkirk*." Jen snorted. "It cost a fortune and it's no good for anything except burning lots of gas." She nudged Kelsie's shoulder. "Now *that's* the kind of boat I like—a real Cape Islander."

With a gasp, Kelsie realized it was Gabriel's white and turquoise fishing boat coming into the dock. She was festooned with orange fishing floats and Gabriel was in the bow, waiting to jump ashore with the rope in his hand—standing like a warrior, head thrown back, shoulders squared.

She hadn't told Jen about meeting Gabriel. Too embarrassing. "I thought you said there weren't any more boats like that," she said.

"That's the Peters' lobster boat. In lobster season they make a lot of money—right now they go out fishing for bait." Jen spoke in her quick, breathless way. "Hardly anybody has a lobster license—they're so hard to get. The guy driving the boat is Guy Peters. That's his son, Gabriel, in the bow."

Kelsie let her own breath out. "I've met Gabriel." She described how he hauled her off the Grinder and out of the ditch.

Jen's blue eyes widened in astonishment. "You've only been in town three days and already you've been rescued by the town hunk ... *twice*!"

Kelsie sighed. "Both times I felt like a total idiot." She looked over at Gabriel leaping ashore in one graceful move. "How old is he?"

"Seventeen." Jen poked her in the side. "I guess you think *he's* cute, right?"

"Maybe," Kelsie agreed.

"He's nice, too … quiet … shy. All the girls in Dark Cove are in love with him, but he doesn't have a girlfriend."

"Are you in love with Gabriel Peters?" Kelsie asked Jen.

"Nah."

"Why not?"

"Well, we're kind of cousins way back—the Morriseys and the Peters. But we're friends. Do you want to talk to him?" Jen was looking at her with laughter in her blue eyes.

Kelsie twisted her tangled curls into a knot at the back of her neck. "No!" she burst out, then, "Yes! I'd like to ask him something."

"Come on." Jen stood up and grabbed Kelsie's hand. She glanced shyly at Andy, still circling in the shallow water near shore. "Do you think Andy would like to meet him?"

"Sure." Kelsie waved to her brother. "We're going over to the long pier," she shouted. "Meet you there."

Gabriel was bending over, coiling rope into a perfect circle on the deck of his boat when they arrived. Other men were loading large blue tubs onto the back of a pickup.

"Hi, Gabe." Jen danced up to the boat. "You already know Kelsie MacKay, and that's her brother Andy in the dory." She pointed to Andy's boat coming toward them.

"Did you get back to your aunt's with your bike okay?" Gabriel's smile was warm and kind and teasing at the same time, Kelsie thought. She felt her knees buckle. It was going to be hard to stay mad at him!

"That—that's a nice looking boat," she gulped.

"Thanks. She's called the *Suzanne*, after my mom."

"Do you ever take it out near Saddle Island?" Kelsie took a step forward.

Gabriel nodded. "Sure. We use the high cliff on the north end of Saddle Island—the Saddle Horn—as a beacon every time we come into harbor."

"Oh, I'd love to go there. The island belongs to our family…." The words were out before she could stop them. She didn't want to seem to be begging Gabriel to take her out to see Saddle Island in his lobster boat.

But if Gabriel thought she was hinting at such an idea, he didn't show it. He and Andy were already into a discussion of fishing for mackerel.

Kelsie wondered why Jen suddenly went quiet and headed back to the Ridout dock where she'd left the *Seahorse*. Had she embarrassed her, talking to Gabriel like that? Or was it something to do with the island?

@ @ @

Jen paddled furiously toward the beach. So Kelsie and her brother knew about Saddle Island. Kelsie would *love* to go there. It belonged to *her* family!

"Well, it's *my* special place, *my* place," Jen said to the rhythm of the paddle. "And Kelsie and Andy will be gone soon. Back to where they came from. Both of them."

She found herself unexpectedly sad at that thought. Kelsie was the best friend she'd had in a long time— a different kind of friend. She'd never care what kind of house you lived in, or the clothes you wore, or your family's hard luck. And Andy. Andy was quieter, more thoughtful than his sister. He wouldn't be so easy to get to know. She wondered if she'd have time to get to know him better—before he left. And then she realized she was half-hoping they wouldn't leave at all—at least not too soon.

@ @ @

On her way back from the fish plant pier, Kelsie decided to take a look inside the barn behind Aunt Maggie's house. She was still thinking about Caspar, shut in his stall.

The barn was small, but well-built, covered in the same weathered cedar shingles as the fish house. Once, her family had owned a farm with horses and kept them in that barn!

She pried open the double doors and stepped in. The barn still had the faint smell of hay and grain, but the bins and stalls were swept clean and bare.

What a perfect place to keep a horse! There was a hay wagon, still with wisps of hay in the cracks between the floor-boards. On the wall, ancient harnesses hung from a nail.

Kelsie went over to touch the stiff leather. A little saddle soap and they could be like new.

She climbed up on the seat of the wagon, imagining the reins in her hands—two horses harnessed and ready to go.

Caspar could pull a wagon like this. No problem!

Suddenly, she heard a stern voice. "What are you doing up there?"

Startled, Kelsie turned and looked over her shoulder. Her aunt stood in the open doorway. Her head was thrown back and she was clutching her throat as if she'd had a terrible shock.

"I … I'm just exploring," Kelsie stammered. "This is such a beautiful barn, Aunt Maggie. It would be so great to have a horse here …"

Her aunt broke in. "Stop! Looking after two kids is enough trouble without animals. Get down from there and come in the house." Her voice was unsteady. "There's something I want to show you."

Wondering what was wrong, Kelsie hopped down from the wagon seat and followed her aunt across the grass to a side door of the blue house. It led to a glassed-in veranda with white blinds covering the windows.

Aunt Maggie went up three steps and opened the door. "This is my room." Aunt Maggie ushered Kelsie in. "It used to be a sun porch, long ago."

Inside, Kelsie saw a single bed with a white bedspread, white walls and a bare plank floor. The only color in the room was the rug her aunt was hooking on the table. Bright strips of cloth overflowed baskets on the floor.

Under the windows were low white bookcases. "Books!" Kelsie exclaimed. No wonder there were none in the rest of the house. They were all here.

"Your father said you liked to read." Aunt Maggie nodded. "But that's not what I wanted to show you." She pulled out an ancient photo album, its cover cracked with age. Quickly she flipped the pages.

"Here … look at this."

Kelsie gazed at the photo of a team of work horses hitched to a hay wagon. There were two kids on the driver's seat and a man standing by the horses' heads.

"That's my dad—your great-grandfather Roland Ridout." Maggie pointed to the man. "He kept a team, even though nobody used horses in the '50s. And that," she went on, "is your grandmother, my sister Elizabeth, when she was fourteen. See what I mean? You're the spitting image of her."

The color was faded, but Kelsie could see that Elizabeth Ridout's hair was reddish brown and curly like her own. Her eyebrows and eyelashes were pale like hers, too.

"That's me." Aunt Maggie pointed to the small dark-haired child. "I didn't like those horses, but wherever Elizabeth went, I had to go, and she was crazy about them. She was full of wild ideas, like running off to the circus and performing on horseback! Later on it was boats …"

Aunt Maggie's face was pale.

"I swear, talking to you it's like my sister is standing here in this room." She put a hand to her forehead. "You see why I was so startled when I saw you on that hay wagon just now. It was like looking at this photograph, come to life."

But I'm not your sister! Kelsie wanted to scream. How was she going to get along with Aunt Maggie when every time she looked at her she saw Elizabeth Ridout? And what on earth had Elizabeth done, Kelsie wondered, that made Aunt Maggie so mad at her?

9

Trail Trouble ◎

For the next three weeks, Kelsie tried to get along with her aunt.

It was hopeless. Aunt Maggie always seemed to be waiting for her to mess up, glaring at her with one raised eyebrow.

Kelsie longed to go to Saddle Island, but she had no chance to ask Gabriel to take her—he was out fishing every day.

"Andy, you could take us in your dory," she begged. "Aunt Maggie will never know, if we pick a time when she's out of the house."

"Aunt Maggie said Saddle Island was too dangerous—remember? She said never to go there." Andy shook his head stubbornly. "I know you. You're just trying to get me in trouble. If I take you to Saddle Island, Aunt Maggie will find out, and I'll lose my motor."

"You're such a wimp!" Kelsie hurled the words at him and Andy stalked away to his boat.

They were both irritable because their dad hadn't written. He called to say he'd arrived safely, and again to say he'd started his job and was working long shifts, but said not a word about moving.

If it hadn't been for Jen and Caspar, Kelsie would have been totally miserable. She spent every day at Harefield Farms.

Finally, at the end of the third week, a check came from their father along with a letter describing the rough diamond mine in the wilderness. They were starting to build houses for the mine workers. He didn't know if they'd be finished before winter set in.

"*Here's some extra cash,*" Kelsie read aloud to Andy in his bedroom. "*One hundred dollars for each of you. Don't spend it all on boats and horses. You'll want new clothes and stuff to start school.*"

Andy threw himself back on his bed with a groan. "School! Why did Dad have to mention *school*?"

"Because it looks like we'll be starting school in Dark Cove in September. It won't be so bad—you'll make new friends." And I'll see Gabriel again, she thought.

"What's the use of making friends? We're not going to be here that long." Andy sat up and looked at her. "We'll be going back to live with Dad in a few weeks. Won't we?"

Kelsie thought it was time to tell her brother the truth.

"Maybe," she answered carefully. "But we might stay here a bit longer. Maybe for a long time."

"I don't want to." Andy frowned. "I want to live with Dad."

"Well, maybe Dad can come here ..." Kelsie suddenly realized she didn't want to move to some lonely northern

mining town. There'd be no horses. No Jen. No Gabriel—
even if he'd already forgotten she existed.

ℚℚℚ

The morning the check came, Kelsie started for Harefield
Farms, dreaming of the new riding boots she'd buy with her
share of the money. Her old ones were too tight.

"If this keeps up," she groaned as she pedaled up the hill,
"I'll be a six-foot-tall, curly-haired giant with enormous feet!"

To her surprise, Jen was tacking up Caspar when she
arrived in the barn.

"Harefield's got important people coming for a trail ride
this afternoon," Jen explained in a rush. "He'll have to use
Caspar because we don't have enough horses."

"That's risky with the mood Caspar's in!" Kelsie exclaimed.
The two of them had done their best to exercise Caspar in the
past three weeks, but he had started chewing his stall door and
was hard to handle. Harefield kept him shut in his stall so he
wouldn't break through fences and escape.

Kelsie strode over to stroke Caspar's snowy nose. She
loved the white horse. Whenever she came to the barn he
would greet her with a special whinny and shove his nose in
her pocket, looking for Aunt Maggie's apples.

Caspar might have some Clydesdale in him, she thought,
with his big head and feathered fetlocks. He was a bit heavy
to ride, but Kelsie couldn't forget their first swim in the ocean.
In the water Caspar felt light and powerful—like floating in
a dream.

"I know I could train him, if he were my horse," Kelsie lamented to Jen. "We have a special understanding, Caspar and I. He'd be fine on the trail today if I rode him."

Jen nodded. "Why don't you ask ..."

But just then, Harefield appeared. He marched toward them, slapping his riding crop on his thigh. Kelsie stifled a laugh. He looked so ridiculous in a cowboy hat and boots, with leather chaps flapping around his chunky legs.

"Jennifer, Kelsie." Harefield's voice rose. "This afternoon the president of the Tourist Association is bringing six tour operators to Harefield Farms. If they like our facilities, we'll have customers from Europe, Japan and all over the world."

He glared at them. "This trail ride must be first-rate, perfect. The future of Harefield Farms depends on it."

Kelsie and Jen glanced at each other out of the corners of their eyes and somehow managed to nod without breaking into snorts of laughter. Harefield's huge hat was sliding over one eye.

But it wasn't so funny when the tour operators rolled up in their silver minivan and the fussiest and most demanding woman insisted on riding Caspar.

Her name was Madame Baretti.

"I *love* white horses," Madame Baretti cooed. "They're so mythical. One thinks of Pegasus, the winged horse of the Gods. So majestic!"

Kelsie glanced at Caspar doubtfully. He was a bit short in the legs and thick through the body to be a mythical flying horse, and he might not behave in a very godlike way, either!

Jen clearly had the same fears. "Are you a … an *experienced* rider?" she asked.

You couldn't very well ask a person if they were any good on a horse without insulting them, Kelsie realized. Especially this woman. Madame Baretti was tall, slender and beautifully dressed in riding jodhpurs and tall black boots.

"Experienced enough," Madame Baretti sniffed. "In any case, your horses should be suitable for all types of riders. That's what we came to find out."

"Of course they're suitable. Gentle as lambs." Harefield glared at Jen. "You won't have any trouble with him." But he looked worried and Kelsie noticed he added a curb chain to Caspar's bit.

Kelsie rolled her eyes at Jen. Harefield was asking for it.

@ @ @

The chattering tour operators set off, out the gate of Harefield Farms along a grassy lane to a trail on the cliffs. Caspar and Madame Baretti rode in front of Kelsie, on Zeke. Jen rode behind, on a black called Midnight.

Kelsie could tell by the sway of Caspar's hind end that he was feeling much too frisky to be moving at this slow pace. Worse, Madame Baretti yanked on his mouth every ten seconds, and Caspar had a tender mouth even without a curb.

Kelsie knew he was just waiting for the chance to bolt, or buck, or do something to get that annoying rider off his back.

Kelsie suddenly remembered a rhyme about a fine lady on a white horse:

"Rings on her fingers and bells on her toes,
And she shall have music wherever she goes."

Kelsie couldn't see if Madame Baretti was wearing rings, but she wasn't going to stay on *that* white horse much longer if she kept hauling on his mouth!

10

Caspar's Disaster ⊚

"Caspar goes better if you keep him on a loose rein," Kelsie called forward to Madame Baretti.

The tall woman turned and gave Kelsie a haughty glare. "I know what I'm doing, thank you very much."

Caspar's ears pricked back at Kelsie's voice as if to say, *"Can't you do anything to help me here?"*

Kelsie bit her lip. They were riding down a steep slope with a small stream at the bottom. It was impossible to keep the horses together. Some went faster on a hillside, some slower. Harefield and a few of the lead horses were already splashing through the stream.

Caspar saw his chance. He bolted out of the line, left the trail and lunged forward at a steep angle with his head thrust down.

Madame Baretti had no chance. She slid forward, lost her balance, flew over Caspar's head and landed with a thud on the hard ground.

Caspar took off with a frisk of his heels and his tail in the air. There would be no catching him, Kelsie knew, not once he was running like that. He was flying, all right—away from the bit in his mouth and the silly woman on his back. Heading for the ocean.

"Stop! Come back here!" Madame Baretti roared, still perched on the ground with her knees bent, waving her arms.

Kelsie threw herself off Zeke's back and ran to help her up.

She saw Harefield glance back in horror, then swing his horse around and come galloping up the trail.

"Oh! My dear Madame, I'm so sorry!"

By this time, Kelsie had managed to get Madame Baretti to her feet. Her immaculate riding pants were soiled red from the Nova Scotia mud. Her pride was bruised more than her body, and she was very angry.

"Your horse deliberately threw me off!" she shouted in Harefield's face. "He's a menace."

Harefield looked down the hill, where Caspar was still running.

"My most sincere apologies, Madame," he cried. "Believe me, Caspar will cease to be a Harefield Farms horse from this moment!"

❧❧❧

"It wasn't Caspar's fault," Kelsie mourned later, as she brushed him down. "That Madame Baretti didn't know beans about horses."

"Of course it wasn't his fault." Jen looked as if she needed brushing down, too. She was damp from running and her mouth curved down in despair.

They had found Caspar on the beach, as usual, and it had been a struggle to get him back up the hill. It was as if the big horse knew what was waiting for him.

Harefield had stomped around shouting and giving orders—Caspar was to be locked in his stall and not let out for any reason. If he got ground into fertilizer, Harefield didn't care. He was getting rid of that horse once and for all!

Jen gulped, "Harefield's sending him to auction this Saturday. The truck comes on Friday. That's four days from now!"

Each word seemed to jab at Kelsie's heart. "What are we going to do?" She turned to Jen with the soft brush in her hand. "Listen. Dad sent me a hundred dollars, and I know he'd send more to save Caspar. We could buy him if we just had a place to keep him …"

"Don't—look at me," Jen despaired. "Mom always says she can barely make enough to feed me, let alone a horse."

"But this is an emergency! I could pay for food. Couldn't we just keep him at your place?"

Jen sighed again, a sigh that went all the way down to her rubber boots. "Our house is on a bare rock. There's no grass, no barn, no fence."

"While my Aunt Maggie has a great little barn with nothing in it!" Kelsie thumped her shovel on the stall floor, startling Caspar. "If only she weren't so weird. Oh! Speaking of my weird aunt—what's the time?"

"Four-thirty." said Jen, glancing at her watch.

"I have to go. Aunt Maggie gets mad if we're late for dinner.

But I'll be here early tomorrow morning, and we'll think of a plan."

She went over to hug Caspar's big white head. "Goodbye, Caspar, you goof. Don't worry, we're going to get you out of here."

"How are we going to do that?" Jen groaned.

❧ ❧ ❧

Biking down the steep hill to the cove, Kelsie saw the flash of a turquoise and white hull coming through the islands.

Gabriel's boat! It looked so beautiful. And Gabriel—she remembered the way he looked standing on the deck of the *Suzanne* ... talking about Saddle Island.

Suddenly, Kelsie screeched to a stop with her new brakes. She shaded her eyes and stared out to sea.

Saddle Island—that could be the answer! Saddle Island belonged to Aunt Maggie, but she never went near it. Her Ridout great-grandparents must have logged and plowed and farmed the island, all with horses. There must be a barn, and pastures ...

Kelsie got back on her bike and pedaled faster. No one would know if they hid Caspar on Saddle Island. He'd be safe there.

And Gabriel could help!

She rolled into the yard of the blue house and threw her bike against the trunk of the apple tree. Late! Andy and Aunt Maggie would already be at the dinner table and she'd get one of those looks—like she could never do anything right.

Sure enough, her aunt gave Kelsie a sharp glance as she burst through the door.

"Sorry, Aunt Maggie," she apologized. "We had some trouble at the barn."

"I'm not surprised," Aunt Maggie sniffed. "I heard Hank Harefield was trying to impress some tourist big shots today. He's always got some scheme to change things in the Cove. I wish he'd give it up and leave the place alone. We're fine as we are."

Kelsie looked carefully at her aunt's angry face. Aunt Maggie hated Harefield almost as much as she did. Should she ask her to help save Caspar?

Too big a risk, she decided. What if Aunt Maggie refused to let her buy him? In that case, Kelsie thought, they'd just have to kidnap him. Better to do it themselves, secretly, without Aunt Maggie knowing a thing.

11

Jen's Decision @

Jen was sweeping straw and dirt from the center aisle when Harefield stormed in next morning.

"Don't forget, that wretched horse goes on Friday." He threw Caspar a nervous look and marched on out.

Forget? How could she forget? Jen thought. She'd been here when the auction truck came to pick up horses. She'd seen them packed together, frightened, suffering, with no hope in their eyes. It had been such a terrible sight she'd had to run from the barn and not watch while Harefield Farms horses were loaded. This couldn't be happening to Caspar.

It wasn't fair!

A few minutes later Kelsie ran into the barn, her cloud of dark red hair flaming around her head like a fierce halo.

"I saw Gabriel last night, coming into the harbor." She paused to catch her breath. "We have to talk to him."

"Gabriel!" Jen stopped sweeping. "What does *he* have to do with this? You see your dreamboat and you forget all about Caspar. Is that it?"

"Of course not. I wouldn't forget Caspar if Gabriel Peters was the whole Olympic hockey team!" Kelsie strode to Caspar's stall. "But I have a *great* idea."

Caspar poked his head out to look at her with a sorrowful brown eye.

"What idea?" Jen asked breathlessly.

"We can take Caspar to Saddle Island. It used to be a farm. But nobody goes there now—it's been deserted for years."

Jen put her head down and started sweeping again. "Saddle Island …?"

"That's where Gabriel comes in," Kelsie rushed on. " We smuggle Caspar on board his lobster boat and he ferries us out to the island. The *Suzanne*'s big enough, and it has that long flat deck at the back."

"Are you kidding?" Jen rolled her eyes. "Gabriel's lobster boat? That's like asking him to drive a pig somewhere in his Porsche. He'd laugh at you."

"Really?" Kelsie straightened Caspar's forelock so it wasn't in his eyes. "Too bad. Saddle Island sounds perfect for keeping a horse."

Jen's heart felt pulled in two directions. It *was* a good idea—but Saddle Island! Kelsie hadn't talked about the island for three weeks and Jen hoped she had forgotten all about it.

Suddenly, Kelsie spun around. "Wait a minute!" she cried. "Maybe we don't need a boat—Gabriel's or anyone else's. Caspar loves to swim. Every time we're near the ocean he fights to get to the water." She pressed her cheek against his. "He could swim from one island to the other till he got to Saddle Island."

"By himself?" Jen said doubtfully.

"Well—no. We could swim with him, on his back."

"People are going to see us."

"Not if we go at night ..." Kelsie's excited voice sank. This was starting to sound wildly impossible, even to her.

"Don't say anymore." Jen hissed. "Here comes Harefield."

"Working hard?" Harefield cast a suspicious eye on them as he strode up the center aisle. "Not thinking of taking Caspar out, are you? I don't want any more trouble with that horse till the auction truck picks him up."

"No, sir," Jen said meekly. "We're just keeping him company."

"We'll see he doesn't get into any more trouble," Kelsie promised.

"Good." Harefield fixed his eye on her. "Did you want a lesson today, young lady?"

Kelsie gulped, "I don't think so. But I'd like to go for a trail ride, if Jen could come, too?"

Harefield regarded them with his head thrown back and his eyes squinted.

"All right," he finally said. "Zeke and Midnight need exercise. Take them, but don't be gone too long." He turned and stalked out of the barn.

"Let's go," Kelsie whispered. "The last thing I want right now is a trail ride! Once we get Caspar out of here I want to stay as far away from Harefield Farms as I can! But I don't want horrible Harefield to know how I feel—I don't want you to lose your job. We'll be able to talk on the trail."

Jen hung up her broom. The mention of the auction truck had brought the horror back. It was coming for Caspar on Friday!

இஇஇ

A narrow horse path wound north from Harefield Farms along the cliff above the shore. Behind Kelsie and Jen was Dark Cove. Ahead was a series of small coves and bays stretching along the eastern shore of Nova Scotia.

Zeke was a good-natured horse as long as Kelsie didn't push him. He was used to the trail and followed Midnight peacefully.

They stopped at a spot high above the ocean and looked back. From this angle, Kelsie could see that Saddle Island was not as close as it looked from Dark Cove. It was the farthest out of three islands.

On one end a high cliff stuck up like a saddle horn. That must be Gabriel's beacon, Kelsie thought, imagining him bringing his boat into harbor on a stormy day.

She tried to picture swimming Caspar across those stretches of icy water and shivered. "Is it better to go at low tide, when the water's not so deep?" she asked Jen.

Jen turned in her saddle. "Are you still thinking about that crazy plan to kidnap Caspar and swim him out to Saddle Island?" she lashed out. "You think it's like swimming in a lake! You don't know anything about the tides and the currents out there."

"But *you* do!" Kelsie argued. "You could swim with him."

There was a pause. Jen looked out to sea and the wind blew her fine hair back from her face. "What makes you think Harefield would sell Caspar to you?" she asked in a low voice.

"Why wouldn't he?" Kelsie insisted. "And why even tell him?" She had been thinking about this. "We could just take Caspar, leave Harefield some money, and if he wants more, pay him after."

"That sounds like stealing." Jen turned to face her.

"Look, Jen, we don't have much time." Kelsie's green eyes were wide. "Today is Tuesday. Caspar goes on Friday. If you can think of a better way to save Caspar, then let's hear it. Otherwise, help me work this idea out, because there's no way I'm going to let Harefield ship him off to the auction as if he was a useless hunk of meat!"

Jen was silent for a moment, gazing at the cliff top on Saddle Island—her secret refuge.

"All right," she said at last. "At low tide there are too many slippery rocks for Caspar to cross. At high tide, he can swim right up to the shore."

"So we'll have to pick a time when it's dark, and high tide …" Kelsie was figuring. "We'll need a good plan."

"I can see one monster problem already," Jen sighed. "Even if I manage to swim Caspar safely to shore on Saddle Island, how will I get back to the mainland?"

"Oooh." Kelsie reached down and patted Zeke's glossy neck. "I hadn't thought of that."

She clucked and Zeke moved ahead down the trail. "I know," she cried, filled with sudden inspiration. "Andy can come and get you in his boat!"

"Why would he do that?" Jen asked.

Kelsie grinned at her over her shoulder. "Oh, he'll do it—if *you* ask him."

@@@

"I'm not going along with any of Kel's goofball schemes." Andy looked shyly at Jen. "I already told her that."

"But we really need you to help us Thursday night," Jen begged. "It's our only chance to save Caspar before he gets carted off to the auction on Friday. "

Andy and Jen were sitting on the dock at sunset that evening. It was low tide. Andy's dory bobbed below them. This was the longest conversation Andy had had with Jen since he met her. He'd wanted to talk to her, plenty of times, but never got his nerve up.

Now, here she was, asking for his help.

"It'll never work." He shrugged. "For one thing, won't Mr. Harefield call the cops on you if you take his horse?"

Kelsie came up behind them and plopped down on the dock.

"I heard that," she said. "Why should Harefield complain? He wants to get rid of Caspar. He says he doesn't care *what* happens to him."

She glanced quickly at Andy. "Anyway, we'll pay him, probably as much as he'd get at the auction."

"How?" Andy scrubbed his spiky blond hair with his knuckles.

"Give him my hundred from Dad and borrow yours ... that'll be two hundred bucks."

"My hundred dollars?" Andy's voice rose to a squeak. "Why should I give you my money?"

"You don't need it right away. Don't worry. I'll ask Dad to send some more for Caspar. I'm sure he will." She tossed back her tangled curls. "After all, he bought you a motor!"

"You win," Andy sighed. "Okay, so you bring that big lump of a horse here. Then what?"

"We'll hide him on Saddle Island. First, Jen swims him to Fox Island, that long skinny one over there, rides across it, swims to Teapot Island—it's tiny –"

Andy's eyes were like saucers. "Wait a minute—*she swims on the horse?*"

"Sure." Kelsie paused, looking down into the water sloshing around the dock timbers. "And then you pick Jen up in your dory."

"I ... pick her up?" Andy could feel himself flushing a deeper red.

"Don't worry. I'll come, too. We'll go at high tide, so you can bring the boat in between the rocks."

"In the dark?" Andy shook his head. "You're nuts. How are we going to do all this running around at night under Aunt Maggie's nose?"

"That won't be easy," Kelsie admitted. "Like I said, we still have some details to work out."

"Details? Huh!" Andy snorted. He was right. This was another of Kelsie's crazy ideas.

"But you'll help us, won't you?" Jen's blue eyes were imploring.

"I don't know—" Andy shifted uncomfortably. "I just don't want to get killed."

"Please," Jen pleaded. "It's an emergency. Maybe we'll come up with a better place to hide Caspar. But right now, Saddle Island is the best we can think of. I'm sure there's plenty of grazing and shelter there." She gestured around the rocky shore. "And you can't hide a white horse on all this dark rock!"

12

Lost at Sea ℗

"All it will take is one tiny squeak on the stairs and Aunt Maggie will be after us like a pit bull," Andy pointed out. "We'll never be able to sneak out at night."

It was getting dark, and time for Jen to go home. The three of them walked up the dock in the gathering shadows.

"What if you didn't sleep inside?" Jen asked. "What if you camped out in the fish house for the night? Maybe I could get permission to sleep over, and we could all bunk in there."

Andy stopped short. "All of us?" he squeaked. "You? Me? And Kelsie? Together?"

"Stop sounding like a twelve-year-old," said Kelsie. "It's a good idea."

She ran up the dock and pushed open the fish house door. It was an old building, damaged by many storms and never repaired. Part of it sat on the dock, part hung out over the water. Inside it was stacked with old nets, eel baskets and fishing gear from the past.

"Look," she pointed up. "Jen and I can sleep in the loft

and you can have the main floor. Will that satisfy your boyish modesty?"

"Freak!" Andy muttered. His ears were as red as his face.

"This place is like a fishing museum." Jen broke into their fight. "They haven't used wooden floats like this for years." She picked up a football shaped piece of brightly painted wood.

"Aunt Maggie keeps everything," sighed Kelsie, "but there is room on the floor for Andy to sleep." She paced the small room. "Now all we have to do is get permission."

᠗ ᠗ ᠗

"Can Kelsie and I camp out in the old fish house Thursday night?" Andy's blue eyes were innocently wide as he took a sip of his steaming cocoa.

Aunt Maggie had made all three of them cups of hot chocolate before bed.

"Of course you can." She sat down on a kitchen chair with a wistful sigh. "Your dad used to spend every summer night in that fish house when he was your age. Wouldn't sleep indoors. He liked to be near the water, near his boat."

"That's it." Andy beamed. "I want to be near my boat."

"I love to look at all the old fishing gear," Kelsie added. "The floats and the nets and the eel baskets—the fish house makes me want to jump in a boat and go fishing!" She was making this up, but as she spoke a strange look came over her aunt's lined face.

"So you can't keep away from the ocean and boats any more than your grandmother …"

Here it was again, Kelsie realized with a shiver, this mystery about her grandmother. It was all right for Andy to sleep near his boat, but somehow wrong for her. That wasn't fair!

"What do you mean, Aunt Maggie?" she asked.

"She had no business going fishing like a boy, leaving her family ashore, but she was mad for the sea. That's what she was. No sense of responsibility…" Aunt Maggie suddenly stopped, her hand on her throat. She shook herself out of her memories. "If you're sleeping in the fish house, you'll need your sleeping bags and flashlights. And you should take water, and some basic food supplies. Your dad used to get so hungry, sleeping outside."

"Thanks, Aunt Maggie," Kelsie murmured. Whatever the mystery was, it would have to wait. At least her aunt had given them permission.

᠗᠗᠗

The next morning, Aunt Maggie took off on a shopping trip to Dartmouth.

"I'd rather you stayed here and didn't go out to Harefield Farms until I get back," she told Kelsie. "I don't want Andy out in that boat while I'm gone."

"All right." Kelsie tried to look disappointed so Aunt Maggie wouldn't get suspicious, but actually she was excited. She would finally have a chance to look through Aunt Maggie's picture albums for photos of Saddle Island.

She headed for the sun porch and found the album she was looking for.

"Andy," she called, "get in here and look at this."

Andy came stomping in with a piece of toast and blackberry jam in his hand.

"Don't get any of that jam on Aunt Maggie's rug or you'll be eating wool strips," Kelsie warned. She held up the album out of reach of his sticky fingers. "I found a picture of the farm on Saddle Island."

The grainy, black and white picture showed buildings with steep roofs and cedar shake walls. There was a house and a small barn, surrounded by a pole fence.

"The fence might still be there—maybe even the house and barn," said Kelsie excitedly. "I can't wait to find out!"

Another photo showed two young girls, side by side on the edge of a small pool. "Aunt Maggie and her sister Elizabeth." Kelsie sighed. "Maybe it's a wishing well and they're making wishes about their future."

Andy plunked down on the floor beside her and stared at the photo of the two girls. "Honestly, Kel, I can't keep it all straight. Is that Elizabeth?" He pointed a finger covered in jam at the taller of the two girls. "Wow! She sure looks like you!"

Kelsie batted his sticky finger away. "Careful! Yes, that's her. She was Dad's mother. She would have been our grandmother if she had lived, but she and our grandfather both died in their thirties."

"Oh." Andy made a face. "Okay, I get it."

"But I still want to know what happened to Elizabeth." Kelsie turned the page. "Look! This is her wedding picture. Why is it stuck in here?"

Among the snapshots of the island was a framed photo of a smiling young woman in a wedding dress and a handsome young man in a tux, cutting a cake. Under the picture was some hand lettering in silver ink:

Elizabeth Ridout and Michael MacKay.
Married June 12, 1964.
Lost at sea off Saddle Island June 12, 1979.

"Lost at sea?" Andy looked up at Kelsie. "What does that mean?"

"It means our grandparents drowned," Kelsie gulped, feelings pouring through her. "They drowned near Saddle Island on their wedding anniversary. How awful! No wonder Aunt Maggie doesn't want to talk about it."

She closed the album. "I wonder how it happened? Maybe we can find out when we get to the island with Caspar."

13

Sudden Plan Change ◎

"Just make sure the motor's running and you've got enough gas in the tank for the trip," Kelsie warned Andy before biking out to Harefield Farms that afternoon. "And check the weather forecast for tomorrow night."

Andy nodded, but he looked worried. "I've already checked the weather. There's a storm coming. And I've never taken the boat out so far—never mind in the middle of the night."

"Jen will tell us where to go. She knows the Cove—we'll be fine." Kelsie promised, hoping she was right.

◎ ◎ ◎

Jen was pacing back and forth in the barn, waiting for her. "I thought you'd never get here!"

"What's happened?" Kelsie could tell by the look on Jen's face that there was more bad news. Caspar, shut in his stall, snorted and shook his head as if to say, *"Get me out of here, or else."*

"We're working on it, big fella." Kelsie reached up to scratch Caspar between the ears.

"We'll have to work faster," Jen groaned. "Caspar kicked at his stall all night and nearly broke down the door trying to get out." She showed Kelsie the splintered wood.

"If he wrecks the stall, I'm scared Harefield won't wait till Friday to get rid of him. He said if he keeps him awake again with his thumping he'll put a bullet through his brain!"

"Harefield said that?" Kelsie gasped. "Then we can't wait till tomorrow, Jen. We'll have to get Caspar out of here tonight."

"Tonight?" Jen gasped. "Do you really think we can do it?"

Kelsie nodded. "We'll have to change our sleepover plan, that's all. You go to work. I'll try to settle Caspar down."

ⓔ ⓔ ⓔ

While Jen did her barn chores, Kelsie kept Caspar company. She groomed him, petted him and talked to him. She couldn't let anything bad happen to him—he was depending on her.

"You've been cribbing." Kelsie rubbed her fingers along the damp chewed wood at the top of his stall door. "Don't you know that chewing wood is bad for you?"

She worried what would happen once they opened that stall door tonight. If Caspar bolted or kicked, she and Jen could never hold him. She remembered how he'd dragged her up to her Aunt Maggie's house in the fog, and how he'd charged into the ocean. You might as well try to hold back a bulldozer!

"We're taking a big chance trying to rescue you," she told Caspar sternly. "You're going to have to help."

By five o'clock, they'd run out of excuses to hang around the barn. Jen rinsed off her barn boots with a hose while Kelsie went over their new plan. Both of them had butterflies in their stomachs thinking of the things that could go wrong.

"Andy and I will meet you at the fish house after supper. Don't forget to ask your mom to let you sleep over tonight," Kelsie said.

"I won't." Jen glanced up at her with worried blue eyes. "She'll say yes if it's all right with your Aunt Maggie ... but you didn't tell her *I* was staying in the fish house with you and Andy, did you?"

"No, I thought she might say no," Kelsie admitted.

"Well, all I can say is, I hope your aunt and my mom don't compare notes."

"I know. It's risky."

❧ ❧ ❧

Coming out of the barn a few minutes later, Kelsie almost ran into Harefield, barging through the barn door.

"Is Caspar behaving himself?" the short man grunted.

"He's pretty quiet now," Kelsie gulped.

"Did you see what that brute did to my stall?" Harefield puffed out his cheeks.

I wish you were in a stall—I'd like to keep you locked up for days, Kelsie wanted to say, but she bit her tongue and just nodded.

"Well, the wretched beast won't be with us much longer," Harefield mumbled.

He had something terrible in mind for Caspar! Kelsie thought as she wormed past him and ran for her bike. They just had to get him out of there before it was too late.

Pedaling hard back to the Cove, Kelsie worried about Andy. Would he be ready with his boat?

Everything depended on that.

@ @ @

"Is the dory ready to go?" Kelsie whispered to her brother as they slid into their places at the kitchen table. "We have to go tonight."

"*Tonight!* Why?" Andy croaked in surprise.

Before Kelsie could whisper a reply, Aunt Maggie came marching toward them with two heaping plates of food.

"Fried cods' tongues and potatoes," she announced. "Your father's favorite."

"Fried *cods' tongues*! Wow!" Andy looked sick.

Actually, Kelsie thought, as she chewed, they tasted like fried onions if you ate them fast.

"We'd like to sleep in the fish house tonight," she told her aunt as she gulped down another cod tongue. "So fried fish is the perfect meal."

"So soon?" Aunt Maggie frowned. "I wish you'd given me more notice. I wanted to fill a cooler with food and supplies for you and Andy."

"I'll help, after dinner." Kelsie volunteered quickly. "We can do it fast."

Aunt Maggie gave her "the look," as Kelsie called it. "Fast isn't always the best," she scolded, then sighed. "But maybe it's just as well. Weather's supposed to turn nasty tomorrow, I heard on the radio. Big storm coming from the south. But don't worry, this evening should be fine. There's a full moon."

Kelsie put down her fork and took a deep breath. It was a good thing they were going tonight!

"I like to watch the moon on the water," Aunt Maggie sighed, as they washed down the last of the fried cod tongues with milk. "I'll come down to the dock later—just look in and make sure you're settled."

Kelsie drew a quick breath of alarm. *She's going to check on us. She'll see Jen!*

@ @ @

It was after ten o'clock when Andy gave the signal, "Look out. Aunt Maggie's coming."

Jen dived under a heap of fish nets in a corner of the loft.

"Well, Andrew." Aunt Maggie shone her flashlight on Andy. "You look cozy." He was stretched on the floor in his sleeping bag.

Aunt Maggie closed the door and walked toward the ladder to the loft. "How is it up there?"

"*Very* cozy," Kelsie murmured sleepily, although sleep was the last thing on her mind! She felt nervous, excited—but not sleepy!

"Well, if you get scared or lonely, come back to the house," advised Aunt Maggie. "I'll leave the back porch unlocked for you."

"Thanks, Aunt Maggie," Andy said. "See you at breakfast."

When Aunt Maggie had gone, Jen wriggled out from under the net. "Do you think she'll come back?"

"Hope not," Kelsie murmured. "It's already so late! If we don't leave soon, we'll never get Caspar back here in time to catch the high tide."

She crept over to a small square window in the loft. "We can see Aunt Maggie's light in the sun porch from here. When it goes out, it'll be safe to leave."

The minutes ticked by. Below them, on the fish house floor, Andy began to snore.

Jen nudged Kelsie's arm. "Think we'll be able to wake him up when it's time to go?"

Kelsie shook her head in the dark. "Let him sleep until we get back with Caspar. If Aunt Maggie does check, she'll peek in and hear Andy snoring like a hippo. I don't think she'll notice I'm gone."

The sun porch light finally blinked out.

Kelsie shone the flashlight on her watch and frowned. "Eleven forty-five. Let's go. We have to be back here and in the water with Caspar by twelve-thirty at the latest."

They stole down the ladder and tiptoed to the door.

Jen shone the light back briefly on Andy's rosy face. "He sure looks cute when he's asleep."

"Come *on!*" Kelsie urged. "Someday I'll tell you about some of my brother's disgusting habits and you won't think he's so cute! But not now. Now we have to ride like the wind."

14

Kidnapping Caspar ❧

They rode with their bike lights switched off. The full moon lit the road. Even the shapes of houses and trees stood out clearly in the moonlight.

At the top of the hill, Kelsie turned for a quick glimpse of the Cove.

The moon sat just above the ocean, throwing a silver path across the dark water. "The moon will help guide us to Saddle Island," Kelsie whispered to herself.

By the time she reached the Harefield Farms gate, Jen had already stashed her bike.

"Shove your bike through this hedge, Kel." Jen pointed the beam of light from her flashlight at a bank of cedars. "There's a ditch on the other side."

Kelsie shoved her bike through the branches.

The barn was in darkness as they ran toward it. There was no sound of Caspar kicking at his stall or neighing to get out.

Kelsie felt a cold fear clutch at her heart. What if Harefield had already done something to silence Caspar—taken him away, or worse?

Inside, the barn was fragrant, silent, as if waiting for something to happen.

Kelsie and Jen hurried toward Caspar's stall, their feet making soft pats on the old plank floor.

Suddenly they heard a snort.

Kelsie clutched Jen's arm. "Caspar! Come on, hurry."

When Jen shone her pocket flashlight on Caspar they saw why he wasn't kicking.

Harefield had hobbled his feet so he could barely move.

With rising fury, Kelsie opened the stall door a crack and hurried to his side. "Poor boy. Don't worry." She bent to untie the knots in the ropes around his legs. "We're getting you out of here."

While Kelsie worked to free Caspar's feet, Jen ran to open the double doors at the end of the barn closest to his stall.

Kelsie heard them creak open. Every sound was magnified in the silence of the barn.

Now if she could just hold this thundering lump of a horse! They had planned to lead him quietly down the road to the shore. But now their time was so short.

"Jen!" she whispered. "Change of plan."

"What?" Jen's flashlight bobbed back to the stall.

"Could you ride Caspar bareback to the beach? It would be faster and I could follow you on my bike."

"Oh! I don't know." Jen focused her flashlight beam away

from Caspar's sensitive face. "He goes so fast, and I won't be able to see the road. What if a car …"

"The moon's out. And Caspar can see in the dark." Kelsie sucked in her breath. She knew what she was suggesting was dangerous.

Caspar was quivering with eagerness—waiting to burst from the stall when the door opened. Kelsie could feel his pent-up power flowing through his body into hers. She latched a lead rope to Caspar's halter and took a firm grip so he had no room to pull.

"I'll ride him if you don't want to!" she cried in a hoarse whisper.

"No." Jen shook her head. "I'd better do it. I know the road, and I've ridden him bareback dozens of times. Lead him out so I can get on. Careful."

Taking a deep breath, Kelsie tightened her grip as Jen swung wide the stall door.

"Just don't get any wild ideas," Kelsie told Caspar firmly. "I'm in charge here." Caspar weighed more than ten times as much as she did, but there were times when it was mind over matter with horses, and this was one of them.

Caspar clattered to the center hall and stood like a statue while Jen stepped up on an overturned manure bucket and sprang to his back.

"Wish I had some reins," she gasped as she dug her hands into his mane and gripped it firmly. They had decided that kidnapping a horse Harefield didn't want was okay, but taking his bridles or saddle was definitely stealing.

Jen got a firm grip with her knees and hands. Kelsie unsnapped the lead rope and hooked it to the side of his halter. She handed the end of the short rope up to Jen. "It's not reins, but it'll help."

Released like a rocket from a launch pad, Caspar leaped into the darkness beyond the barn doors.

Kelsie just had time to yank an envelope out of her pocket and stuff it in the hay net in the corner of Caspar's stall. She dashed out of the barn, tore across the stable yard, dragged her bike out of the ditch and took off after Caspar's galloping hooves, already far down the road.

She didn't look back.

ᘒᘒᘒ

Harefield snapped awake to the sound of hooves thudding down his driveway. He shot out of bed and reached for his rifle.

"CASPAR!" he shouted. "If that horse is loose again, I'll —"

Throwing on some clothes, he hurried downstairs, flicked on the yard lights and ran to the barn.

Caspar's stall gaped open. Not stopping to look inside, Harefield ran back to the yard and jumped in his pickup truck. "I'll get him, I'll get him," he shouted. "He's run away from this barn for the last time!"

The truck's engine roared into life. With clashing gears and screaming tires, Harefield rocketed out of the driveway and down the road. No need to wonder where Caspar was heading—he'd be galloping straight for the sea!

Kelsie heard the racket of the pickup behind her before the lights swept around the curve and caught her in their beam.

She just had time to steer for the ditch.

Harefield's truck! Kelsie saw the Harefield Farms lettering on its side as the truck sped past. She rolled over, aching from the sudden impact with the grass and dirt. I'll bet this is the same place I hit the ditch when my stupid brakes failed and Gabriel had to rescue me, she thought bitterly, spitting out sand.

That didn't matter. Harefield had heard them—he was chasing Caspar!

Kelsie yanked herself and the bike up the bank of the ditch. If only Jen heard him in time to get Caspar off the road! The way Harefield was driving, he was in a dangerous rage.

☙☙☙

Caspar's keen ears heard the truck before Jen's. He let out a loud whinny of warning, snorted and threw up his head.

"What's wrong?" Jen cried, and then heard the rattle of the truck, coming fast!

Before she could steer Caspar off the road it screeched to a halt behind her.

Jen heard Harefield shout, "Stop! Come back!"

But there was no way she was stopping. "Come on, Caspar, we've got to get out of here!" She pummeled him with her heels. With a mighty leap, Caspar soared over the ditch and raced across the backyards of Dark Cove.

The full moon lit their way over low fences, rocks and gardens, past houses and sheds, heading down toward the water.

Caspar was enjoying this wild ride. He could see clearly, even without the moon. But Jen kept her head low, hugging Caspar's neck, fearful of clotheslines or telephone wires strung across their path. If she hit one of those, she'd be headless on this horse!

ⓠ ⓠ ⓠ

Andy was still snoring when Jen reached the door of the fish house and slid from Caspar's broad back.

"Andy?" she called. "Andy, wake up." She shoved the door open with one hand.

Andy still droned away on the floor, deep asleep.

"Come on, Caspar." Jen led him through the door. He clopped across the wood floor, filling the small shed with his bulk.

"Andy?" Jen called again.

Caspar, puzzled by the sound and smell of a human stretched on the floor, bent his large white head and blew in Andy's face.

"Wha—What!" Andy's flash snapped on. "Oh, cripes! What's that? Ow! Get him off," he spluttered.

Caspar backed off with a startled snort.

"Quiet!" Jen warned. "I had to wake you up somehow."

"Why? Where's Kelsie?" Andy shone his flashlight around the fish house.

"I ... I don't know. She *was* coming on her bike. But

Harefield heard us and came after us in his truck. We'll have to hide Caspar in here till he's gone." Jen pleaded with Andy. "Don't say I told you so. Just help."

"Okay, but phew! What a terrible way to wake up. I dreamed a smelly monster was trying to bite my nose."

"Caspar was curious." Jen grinned in the flashlight's beam. "I don't think he ever heard snoring before."

"Snoring? Was I?" Andy gulped. "Sorry." He tried to squirm to his feet, but Caspar was standing on his sleeping bag.

"Get him off my bed!" he shoved at Caspar.

The horse gave a nervous jump and lunged into the wall of rickety shelves.

"No! Caspar!" Jen screamed in a whisper. Too late. The shelves collapsed, throwing floats, nets and heavy tools onto Jen and the horse.

15

Ice-cold Water ⊚

"Jen!" Andy scrambled to his feet. "I'm sorry! I didn't mean to make Caspar jump like that."

"Not your fault," murmured Jen through gritted teeth. "I think he's okay."

"But what about you?" Andy ran to help her out from under the rubble.

"The shelf hit my shoulder when it collapsed," Jen groaned. "I think it's just bruised ... not broken."

"Stupid horse!" Andy glared at Caspar.

"Not his fault, either. He's just too big for the fish house, but I had to bring him here ..."

Jen paused. "Listen!"

They heard footsteps coming down the dock.

"Harefield!?" Jen whispered.

"Or my Aunt Maggie?" Andy realized they'd been making a lot of noise.

The door burst open. "Are you in here? Are you all right?"

It was Kelsie.

"We've got to hurry," Kelsie panted. "Horrible Harefield's driving like a maniac all over Dark Cove, looking for Caspar. I had to dodge him about six times."

She stopped, staring at the chaos on the fish house floor, and Jen, still on her knees, holding her shoulder. "What happened in here? Jen! What's wrong?"

"Caspar fell against the shelves and they collapsed," Jen groaned. "I've wrenched my right shoulder. I don't think I'll be able to hold him in the water."

"Poor you!" Kelsie ran to crouch by her side. "Don't worry. I'll swim him to the island."

"You don't know the route or the currents." Jen shook her head. "It will be too hard for you."

Andy shone the light on his watch. "Anyway, it's past twelve-thirty. Our schedule's already off. I say we abort this mission."

Kelsie jumped up, grabbed her brother's arm and swung him to face her. "Listen, Andy. This isn't a video game. Harefield's hunting for Caspar all over town. For all we know, he's got his rifle with him. Saddle Island is Caspar's best chance."

"But Andy's right," Jen gasped, as she got painfully to her feet. "If we don't leave right now, it will be too late to catch the tide."

@ @ @

A few minutes later they were on the shore below Aunt Maggie's dock with Caspar.

The wind was blowing hard and the sound of the surf on the beach boomed in their ears.

Andy's dory swung on its rope nearby, loaded with supplies.

"I'm ready." Kelsie shivered in her bathing suit. The night under the full moon was cool. The water, when she stuck her toe in, was like ice.

"Here." Jen rummaged in her duffel bag and dragged out a black mass. "Put this on—it's my mom's wet suit." She flattened out the one-piece rubber suit. "She uses it to go body surfing when the ocean is freezing—like now."

"I don't want to wear this!" Kelsie held up the wet suit. "It feels disgusting."

"Listen, Kelsie," Jen spoke in a serious voice Kelsie hadn't heard her use before. "Try it on. You might be in the cold water a long time and that's dangerous."

"Come on, Kel," Andy argued. "Jen knows a lot more about this ocean stuff than you do. Wear the suit."

"All right, I'll try ..." The rubber felt cold and clammy against Kelsie's skin. "Ugh," she said. "Now what?"

"The zipper." Jen started it for her. It ran all the way up her body to her neck. "And here are some boots for your feet and a life jacket."

"I feel strangled." Kelsie wriggled to get the wet suit in place. "And I can't bend."

"Wait till you get in the water—it'll be better." Jen led Caspar forward.

Kelsie pulled on the wet suit booties and life jacket, strapped on a waist pack with her watch, compass and flashlight, stepped on a rock and then onto Caspar's back.

The big horse splashed into the water. *This* is what he'd been waiting for. Kelsie could feel his joy in every toss of his head.

She could also feel the cold creeping into her wet suit. As Caspar swam out from shore, Kelsie felt air puff out from her ankles to her throat. Then all the air was gone. The wet suit hugged her body with warmth. Her hands stung with the cold, and she realized her whole body would have felt like this without it.

The moon made a path to follow. Droplets of water shimmered off Caspar's mane. The powerful muscles of his swimming legs surged beneath her as he swam steadily toward the first island. Kelsie thrilled to the sensation of riding a horse through deep water. She could have swum on that moonlight path forever.

But the shore of the first island, Fox Island, loomed up to her right.

Caspar struggled to keep his footing on the rocks, and lunged for the shore. He clambered up the rocks, water streaming from his hide.

Kelsie's flashlight showed a solid wall of stunted spruce trees. White moss hung from the branches like ghostly lace. She slipped from Caspar's back and checked her compass.

"Keep going straight east," she told herself aloud. In this thick brush it would be easy to get turned around and start going in circles. She knew Fox Island wasn't wide. Fifteen minutes should get them to the other side, even with the thick brush slowing them down.

᠗ ᠗ ᠗

The swim to the second island was short. Teapot Island was really just a bubble-shaped dome of rock. Its few scattered spruce trees were bent and twisted by the wind.

Kelsie shivered as she ran across it with Caspar. The wind cut through her wet suit. Wind, she thought. It's picking up.

This time, Caspar hesitated before plunging into the third stretch of black water. The waves slapped harder on the far side of Teapot Island where the open sea rolled in from the east. The bulk of Saddle Island loomed in the distance, and its high cliffs cut off the moon.

"It's okay, Caspar. Let's go," Kelsie urged. "Just one more channel to cross and you'll be safe on Saddle Island."

As he splashed into the waves, she wondered where Jen and Andy were with the dory. They'd be heading around the south side of the islands, then turning in to land in the sheltered channel Jen described. Somewhere in the channel was a safe landing place.

Kelsie prayed she could find it in the dark water with the wind blowing hard. She clung to Caspar's neck as the sea foam swept over his head.

Lost at sea—the words rang in her ears. My grandmother Elizabeth looked like me and she drowned.

16

Fight for the Shore @

"The boat's leaking!" Jen heard Andy shout from the stern of the dory.

Jen knew how serious this was—forcing the old dory through rough seas at high speed was shaking her to pieces, just as Andy's dad had predicted.

She could see Andy trying to steer with one hand and bail with the other, using a plastic bucket. It was throwing them off course.

In the bow of the dory, Jen tried to get her bearings on the tall island in front of them. They had to hit the channel just right or the wind would blow them out to the open sea.

Jen checked her compass with a flashlight. "A bit more to the left," she shouted to Andy.

"It's hard to keep her headed that way with the wind," he hollered back.

"It's the tide, not just the wind," she yelled. "It makes currents between the islands."

"How much farther?" Andy bellowed.

"I'm not sure. Watch for Kelsie's signal."

"This is my sister's craziest idea yet!" she heard Andy shout. "We're going to sink before we get there!"

Andy was sloshing water over the side. Jen picked up a plastic pail to help, but her shoulder burned with every scoop. "Once we get inside the channel we'll have some protection from the wind," she hollered to give him hope.

"Okay. I'm glad you're with me, Jen. I'd really hate to be out here by myself."

"Thanks, you're doing fine." Jen's shoulder throbbed, but she hardly felt it. It was the first time Andy had said anything about liking her. It didn't bother her that he was scared—she liked him because he was smart and funny and sensible. Anyone who was tossing around in an open boat on that dark ocean—any sensible person—would be terrified!

She hoped Kelsie had reached the shore of Saddle Island. She should be there by now.

@@@

Kelsie knew she had to aim Caspar at a spot between two tall trees in the center of the island.

Jen had told her about a rocky cleft where Caspar could safely come ashore.

They must be close. She could hear waves pounding on the rocks. It was past high tide but Kelsie prayed the water would still be deep enough so that Caspar could swim right into that groove in the rock.

If only it wasn't so dark! If they didn't hit the right place she and Caspar could be dashed against the jagged rocks that ringed the shore. Kelsie felt Caspar's legs falter. He was afraid of the waves booming on the rocks ahead.

Suddenly, the moon soared above Saddle Island and shone down on them like a spotlight. It lit the water with its pale phosphorescence, showing the waves foaming on the shore.

"Just a bit farther," she urged Caspar. "NO! Don't even think about turning back." She pounded him with her heels under the water, knowing he would hardly feel it. "See—the moon's showing us the way!"

With waves swirling around them, she aimed Caspar straight for the groove in the rock. It was carved at an angle, as if some giant ice beast had clawed the edge of the island in the days of an ancient glacier.

Inside its shelter, the water surged in and sucked back. Kelsie swam Caspar to its narrow end. She could feel his feet touch the sand. With a mighty shove he hoisted himself up onto the sloping shelf of rock.

Kelsie slid from his back and leaned against his heaving side. "Good, good Caspar," she shouted above the pounding of the waves. "We're safe on Saddle Island. Just let Harefield and the auction truck try to find you now!"

☙☙☙

The wind drove against Kelsie and the horse on the exposed shore. She led him back from the water's edge and looped his lead rope around the branch of a scrubby spruce.

"I have to go and signal Jen and Andy," she explained to Caspar. "You stay here where it's sheltered."

Shining her flashlight on her watch, she saw that it had taken much longer than they had planned to reach the island. Jen and Andy must be out there, somewhere, waiting for her flashlight as a beacon.

She ran down to the water's edge, flashed the light out to sea one, two, three times and then a pause.

To her astonishment the answering signal came from just a short distance away.

"Hello!" Kelsie shouted into the wind. "Come in slow— the landing place is here." She shone her light on the narrow cleft in the rock.

She heard Andy cut his motor back from full speed to a slow crawl. The boat came into view, with Jen in the front, ready to leap ashore with a rope.

"Good thing you signaled when you did," she called. "We knew we were getting close, but we couldn't see how close! We might have struck the rocks."

Andy killed the motor and rowed closer. "We made it, we made it!" he repeated, shaking his head. "I never want to do that again. The boat is leaking, and it was so rough."

"Andy was great." Jen threw the rope to Kelsie with her good arm and stepped ashore. She pushed back the hood of her slicker and her brown hair caught the moonlight. "How are you and Caspar?" she asked Kelsie breathlessly.

"We're okay. Caspar must be thirsty and hungry though, and tired! I tied him over there …" She stopped, feeling a wet nose nuzzling the back of her neck. "Stop that! Where did you come from?"

Caspar, the escape artist, had managed to get loose and had come to join the group.

17

Spiders and Vines ◉

The big horse followed close at Kelsie's heels while they un-loaded the dory and piled their supplies on the rock. Andy had brought matches to start a fire. They found kindling and chunks of driftwood to build a blaze on a sheltered spit of land.

Kelsie crouched by the fire, warming her frozen hands.

"Good fire," Jen handed Andy a sandwich from the cooler they'd packed.

"My dad taught me to make campfires." Andy looked shyly at her. "He's an expert in the woods."

Kelsie consulted her watch by firelight. "Finish your sand-wich and let's go. We've got to find water and a place to picket Caspar before the sun comes up."

She looked up at Caspar, who was standing just outside the circle of firelight, munching on the leaves of a bush. "As soon as it's light we'll have to head back and hope we make it before Aunt Maggie notices we're missing."

Andy stared at his sister's firelit face. "Are you nuts? We

don't know anything about this island. How are we going to find our way around in the dark?" He shrugged. "Let's stay here by our nice warm fire and let Caspar go find his own food and water."

"We have to tie him up!" Kelsie flared at her brother, as if Andy were a little kid. "Because he'd swim after us if we didn't. And we have to find a place to tie him where he can drink fresh water and graze. Because we're not sure when we can get back to the island. *Do you understand?*"

"Aw …" Andy turned away. "This is all crazy. I'm stuck on a deserted island with two horse lunatics."

Jen stood up and went to his side. "It'll be all right."

"How do you know?" Andy asked crossly and then more gently, "How's your shoulder?"

"Better." Jen rubbed it gingerly.

"Come on, you two, we're wasting time." Kelsie stood up, brushing sand off her pants. "Let's go look for the old Ridout farm. There's bound to be water there."

She ran to the boat, scooped up water with the bailing bucket and threw it on Andy's fire.

It sizzled and went out, leaving them in the moonlight.

☙ ☙ ☙

They set off into the tangle of brush, Jen in front, then Andy, then Kelsie leading Caspar.

It wasn't long before they were stopped by a wall of bushes with sharp thorns. Rustling sounds came from nearby, and the munching of big horse teeth.

"Caspar, what are you eating?" Kelsie shone her flashlight into the tangled vines. Its beam gleamed on huge blackberries hanging from leafy vines. Caspar was ripping off the berries with his large teeth and gulping them whole.

"Blackberries!" Andy cried. "Wow!" He dashed for the bushes. "Ouch, ugh! Yum!" The blackberry thorns were wickedly sharp and came off in his skin.

"Are blackberries good for horses?" Kelsie asked doubtfully.

"Sure." Jen's voice came out of the darkness. "Full of vitamins. "But it's not going to be easy getting through here."

She was right! The vines tangled around their legs, stuck to their jeans and tore their bare hands. Kelsie tried to clear a path with her arm and felt something sticky across her face. She swiped it off—a spider web!

"Watch out for spiders," she warned.

"I know," Andy groaned. "They're everywhere. I think I ate a couple by mistake."

A few minutes later, he stopped, and threw up his arms. "Does anyone know where we're going, or are we just following Caspar? I think we're lost. I think these stories about some old farm are legends. I'll bet the whole island is overgrown like this!"

Kelsie fought down panic. The grasping vines trapped her. "For once, I think you're right," she gasped. "I'm sorry I got us into this—we'll have to go back—I'll have to swim Caspar back to the mainland –"

"No. It's all right. I can find the way." They heard Jen's soft breathless voice in the darkness. She came through into Andy's flashlight beam, her fine hair tangled around her face.

"How?" Kelsie gaped at her, astonished. Jen looked like some woodland sprite that had appeared out of nowhere.

"Look at the ground." Jen shone her pocket flash under the bushes. "See the stones and sand? I think Caspar found an old road." She looked up at them. "It's not the path I usually take, but I'm pretty sure it will lead to the farm."

There was a silence in which all three of them could only hear their breathing and Caspar's peaceful chewing.

Finally, Kelsie asked, "What are you talking about? How do you know so much about this island?"

"Because I come here all the time." Jen let her breath out in a rush. "I imagine it's my own island." She blinked and held her hand up to shield her eyes from Andy's light. "I've never explored this part. I usually take a path along the shore to the Saddle Horn."

"Why didn't you tell us?" Andy moved his flashlight beam away from her face.

"Because Saddle Island isn't really mine—and I didn't want you to think that…. I wanted to go on believing—and then after you moved away, everything would be the same."

"Jen!" Kelsie exclaimed. "Look. Nobody uses this island. It might as well be yours. While Andy and I are here we can share it—if that's okay?"

"Okay," Jen said. "We'd better keep going. Like I said, I think we're on the road to the farm. The blackberry vines have just grown over it."

They slowly made their way deeper into the tangled vines, their flashlights bobbing. Caspar had gone ahead, plunging through the undergrowth.

The sky grew lighter as the time crept close to four o'clock, and they switched off their flashlights. Everything looked ghostly in the gray light. They finally found Caspar, reaching up to nibble berries from vines that climbed an ancient apple tree.

"It's an old orchard!" Jen cried. "We must be near the farm."

She ran forward, forcing her way through the tangle of vines, with Kelsie and Andy right behind her. They almost stumbled into a stone wall.

"I'll bet this was the barn!" Kelsie stroked the rounded stones in wonder. All that was left of it were four stone walls, higher than their heads and pointed at each end.

Jen pointed. "There's a bit of roof on that corner."

They made their way to it through brambles and loose stones.

"The rest of the barn must have burned down," said Andy, picking up a piece of charred wood.

The light was getting stronger. "Let's see what else we can find," Kelsie said.

There wasn't much. A few lilies and late roses showed where a garden once grew. The fences had all fallen down.

Caspar had wandered ahead of them again. They heard deep slurping sounds. "Water!" Jen and Kelsie shouted at the same time and rushed to find him.

In one corner of an old pasture, a spring bubbled up, surrounded by a man-made trough of smooth stones. "The sisters' wishing well." Kelsie breathed a sigh of relief. "It's a perfect place to picket Caspar."

In the rosy dawn light they fixed a picket line with a rope over Caspar's head so he could move freely without getting tangled. He could reach the water, and there were plenty of small trees and berries to nibble.

"You'll be okay for a while." Kelsie hurried to tie the big horse to the line. "Now stay here, Caspar, until we come back. No funny stuff, understand?"

Did he understand, she wondered as they raced back to the dory? Did he understand being left alone on Saddle Island? Somehow, she'd have to talk Andy into coming back with the dory later today. Jen couldn't paddle with a sore shoulder, and she still hadn't had a lesson in the kayak.

Back at the landing, Andy fired up the motor as she and Jen climbed aboard. The tide was going out and the water level on the rock had fallen. The wind was blowing inshore. She and Jen pushed against the rock to keep the dory from banging until they were clear.

The sky behind them was streaked blood red with the dawn.

"Red sky in the morning, sailor take warning," Jen shouted over the roar of the outboard. "It's an old fisherman's saying. A red sky like that means there'll be a storm in twenty-four hours or less."

18

Sunk! @

Hank Harefield stood staring into Caspar's empty stall at six a.m. He'd been up all night, looking for that horse. It was as if Caspar had disappeared into thin air.

His eye caught a flash of white in the hay net.

"What's this—some kind of note?" He ripped the envelope open. Inside were four fifty-dollar bills and a handwritten letter:

> Dear Mr. Harefield,
> We have rescued Caspar. Here is two hundred dollars to make up for what you might have got for him at the auction. We think this is fair.
> Yours truly,
> The Committee Against Cruelty to Caspar

"Oh, you do, do you?" blustered Harefield. "Fair, my eye! You can't steal a man's horse!" He scrunched up the note. "I should have known—it's that Kelsie MacKay—the Ridout woman's niece. Committee Against Cruelty, my eye! We'll see what her aunt has to say about this."

Harefield stuffed the note and the fifty-dollar bills in his pocket and strode angrily out of the empty barn.

@ @ @

The dory made swift time with the wind at its back, but it was leaking worse than ever. The cracks between its boards had widened and water poured in, wetting everything.

Soon, it covered their ankles.

"BAIL!" Andy howled at Kelsie and Jen.

They bailed feverishly, hurling water over the side till their arms ached.

At last they rounded Fox Island, and the Ridout dock was in sight.

The water in the dory was up to their knees.

It was now six-thirty, an hour from low tide, but already rocks poked out of the small bay, glistening with seaweed. Black cormorants perched on the rocks, holding their wings out to dry.

"I can see the bottom," Jen panted. "We're almost there."

But the water was rising faster than they could slosh it out. A few feet from the dock, the dory, motor and all their belongings settled into the sand, with the waves washing over the sides. The seagulls flew overhead, laughing at the sight.

Andy hung his head in despair. "It's wrecked," he moaned. "The dory's a piece of junk and my motor's history."

"But we made the shore." Kelsie splashed over the side with the cooler in her arms. "Hurry! We've got to get all this wet stuff up to the fish house before Aunt Maggie sees us."

It took several trips, but at last all the wet gear was safely stowed under a canvas tarpaulin.

Just in time. They were no sooner back in their sleeping bags than the fish house door creaked slowly open.

Aunt Maggie's face poked in. "Both of you still sleeping?" she asked softly. "Don't be late for breakfast."

Andy made grunting noises. He held the sleeping bag tight under his chin so she wouldn't see his wet clothes.

"We'll be up soon," he mumbled sleepily.

"All right. How was your night?"

"Oh … fine, I guess."

"There was quite a wind. I thought you two might have been frightened." Aunt Maggie paused. "I think you should sleep in the house tonight—they say this storm may blow in worse."

"Umungh …" muttered Andy.

Kelsie waited until she heard the fish house door shut, then sat up and stared despairingly at Jen.

"What are we going to do?" she moaned. "The storm's getting worse. You can't paddle, and the dory's at the bottom of the ocean. How are we going to get back to Saddle Island?"

"Who cares!" Andy shouted from below. "I lost my boat—though neither of you seems to care about that."

Jen climbed down the ladder. "Of course we care," she told Andy. "But we're worried about Caspar. Especially if there's a bad storm."

"I'll get to Saddle Island today if I have to paddle the kayak myself." Kelsie bounded down behind her.

"Don't be stupid." Andy kicked his sleeping bag off his

feet and yawned. "You can't paddle the kayak—especially if there's a storm. Why don't you go in another boat—my friend Gabriel's boat, for instance."

Kelsie seized him by the shoulders. "Since when is Gabriel your friend? We hardly know him."

"*You* hardly know him. I talk to him almost every day, while you and Jen are up at Harefield Farms. He asks about you, too, but I say you're only interested in horses …"

"ANDY!" Kelsie bellowed. "You're making this up."

"Okay, have it your way—I'm making it up." Andy shrugged again. "But all I'm saying is that Gabe takes his boat out past Saddle Island every day. Maybe he could drop us off and pick us up again on the way back."

Kelsie stared at him, stunned.

"That's a good idea." Jen nodded. "Gabriel will go out in anything short of a hurricane—the *Suzanne* is a big strong boat. I'll bet if Andy asks him, he'll say yes."

"Would you do it?" Kelsie's green eyes drilled into Andy's brown ones.

"I might, if you quit squeezing me like a cobra." Andy was still angry at losing his boat and grumpy from lack of sleep.

"I've got to get home and call Harefield Farms and say I'm too tired to come in today." Jen sighed wearily. "I *am* really tired, so it's not a lie. I'll meet you here in about an hour, okay?"

"Okay," Kelsie said, letting Andy go. "And put some ice on your shoulder."

"What if Aunt Maggie notices the dory is gone?" Andy asked, as Jen left.

"She won't. She never goes near the water. And if she does, we'll just say it drifted free and sank in the night." Kelsie took Andy's hand. "If you can get Gabriel to help us, I promise I'll help you raise the dory and get it fixed."

"Sure, after you spent all our money on that horse!" Andy pulled his hand away.

"I'll figure out a way. Will you see him?"

"All right," Andy sighed. "I'll go see Gabe right after breakfast."

As they hurried to the house, Kelsie's brain was reeling. Could it be true that Gabriel asked about her? She could easily believe that Andy wouldn't tell her if he did. He wouldn't even understand how totally important it was!

ଷ ଷ ଷ

"It's about that niece of yours," Harefield stood with his hands on his hips at the edge of Maggie Ridout's garden later that morning.

She scowled up at him from under her wide-brimmed hat. "Kelsie and Andy aren't here."

"I think they've got my horse in your barn." Harefield pointed to the barn's closed doors."

"You mean Caspar? The horse that wanders in and tramples my garden?" Aunt Maggie stood and faced the angry man. She was several inches taller than he was. "It would serve you right if I did catch him and keep him in my barn, but I didn't."

"Do you mind if I check?"

"Yes, I mind!" Aunt Maggie glared down at him. "It's none of your business what's in my barn!"

"It is, if it's my horse!"

"My niece would never take your horse, Mr. Harefield." Aunt Maggie declared. "You're talking gibberish."

"Oh, really? Read this." Harefield thrust the note and fifty-dollar bills at her.

Aunt Maggie read the note and her face turned pink. "This isn't signed."

"But who else except your niece and her friend Jennifer Morrisey would have taken him—it was obviously a child who wrote this nonsense about rescuing Caspar. Jennifer didn't show up for work today—what do you say to that?"

Aunt Maggie threw back her head and said stiffly, "I'd say I haven't seen your horse, but that you're welcome to look in my barn, if you wish."

The two of them marched across the grass to the barn, where Aunt Maggie threw open the double doors. "You see?" she said triumphantly. "There's no horse in here. Hasn't been for fifty years."

Harefield looked like a punctured balloon. "Well, they've taken him somewhere else, then," he muttered. "I'll find them."

"Well, good luck!" Aunt Maggie banged the barn doors shut.

"I guess that takes care of that windbag," she muttered to herself, as Harefield stalked away. But she wondered if Kelsie and Jen were behind Caspar's disappearance.

In the back of Aunt Maggie's mind was the image of four fifty-dollar bills clutched in Harefield's hand. The money from Doug's check for the children had been in fifty-dollar bills. Could Andy be involved in these goings-on, too?

19

Horse Dreams ◎

At that moment, aboard the *Suzanne*, Gabriel Peters checked his watch.

"It's eleven-thirty now." He looked into Kelsie's excited green eyes and grinned his lopsided grin. "Every time I see you you're in some kind of trouble. Try not to get into any more today—I need you back here at this landing by four-thirty. No later."

Gabriel pointed to a vicious line of rocks poking out of the channel between Saddle Island and Teapot Island. "I don't want to get blown onto that old causeway when the tide's going out."

"We'll be here," Kelsie promised. To her delight, Gabriel had agreed to drop them off on Saddle Island. She reached for the backpack of supplies Gabriel handed to her and stepped lightly ashore. Gabriel had steered his boat with such skill that it barely kissed the rock when they landed.

Now he eased the *Suzanne* carefully away from the landing place. The waves spanked at the *Suzanne*'s stern as he backed the boat out toward the open sea.

"Good luck!" he called. "Andy, don't forget to pick a tub of blackberries for me, buddy."

"I won't." Andy held up the empty pail on his arm. He wore a grin on his face from ear to ear.

Kelsie watched until the *Suzanne* disappeared around the corner of the island. Gabriel ... Gabriel! His name and the image of his laughing face filled her mind.

Jen pulled on her sleeve. "Caspar? Remember? We don't have much time."

"Gabe made her forget all about horses," Andy teased. "Now she has a new love."

"Shut up!" Kelsie turned away. She didn't want to be teased about Gabriel. Her feelings were too raw, like a newly bruised knee.

Saddle Island was beautiful in the sunshine. Light gray rocks sloped down to a dazzlingly blue ocean edged with white foam. The blackberry vines that had pricked their skin last night glistened with berries as big as her thumb. Even the spiderwebs were magical—each one outlined in dew.

Andy dived into the nearest berry patch with a shout. "This place sure looks better in the daytime! Hey! Did you know our great-grandfather was a smuggler?" He was trying to talk and eat blackberries at the same time.

"Who told you that?" laughed Kelsie.

"Gabriel. He said Roland Ridout smuggled rum from the Caribbean Islands and hid it right here on Saddle Island. He had a secret hiding place somewhere, called a stash. After I get Gabe's berries I'm going to look for it."

"The way you're eating them, you'll never get that bucket full. We're going to check on Caspar." Kelsie waved goodbye. "Remember what Gabriel said—don't get in any trouble!"

"He meant you, not me!" Andy mumbled with his mouth full.

ම ම ම

They could hear Caspar neigh long before they saw him.

He was protesting the whole idea—being tied to the picket line—left all alone in a strange place.

"It's all right, Caspar, we're here." Kelsie ran to him and took his big head in her hands.

"We only have five hours," she told Jen. "Five hours to make him more comfortable, make sure he has good grazing, and try to fix him a shelter."

"I wish I wasn't so tired!" Jen yawned. "I'm not used to being up all night."

"I'm too scared to be tired." Kelsie hugged Caspar. "I hate the idea of leaving you again, big guy. I hope you'll be all right if the storm is really bad."

"Let's take him off this picket line while we're here." Jen reached up and unclipped the line. "At least he'll get some exercise."

So while they explored the old farm in better light, Caspar followed Kelsie and Jen everywhere they went. Near the ruined barn they discovered the remains of a pole fence and an old pasture. Caspar rolled in the soft grass and whickered with pleasure.

"This is pretty good grazing for you, boy." Kelsie stroked his white neck. "And I don't see any weeds that would make you sick, like ragwort or buttercups. All we need is a new fence."

In one corner of the paddock they found rose hips on a wild rose bush. "These are good for him, too." Jen broke off one of the hard red hips and fed it to Caspar. "Lots of vitamin C."

"So he'll have enough food, at least for now." Kelsie sighed with relief. "Let's check the water."

The spring seeped out of the ground into the rock-lined pool and then trickled off to form a small stream. Kelsie dipped her hand in and drank from it. "Delicious!" she sighed. "This island is a paradise—fresh water, green grass, sea air. No wonder my ancestors settled here. I wish ..."

There was no use wishing she could live there, Kelsie realized. Dad was a hard rock miner and there were no mines in this part of Nova Scotia. Even if she stayed with Aunt Maggie, she'd never convince *her* to set foot on Saddle Island. It was as if there was a curse on the Ridout family—that somehow, through her grandparents' death, they could never return to this island.

She straightened up from the spring. "Let's take a look at the barn," she told Jen. "I'd like to see if we can make a shelter for Caspar to wait out the storm—if it comes."

Jen looked up at the quiet trees. "Not much wind now," she said, "but maybe it's the calm before the storm. If we have time, after we fix the barn, I'll show you my favorite place up on the Saddle Horn. If you want to ..." Her voice trailed off into a sigh.

"Of course I want to," Kelsie grinned. "We're sharing this island, but you were here first, remember?"

Meanwhile, Andy was finally full of berries. In fact, his stomach hurt, he'd eaten so many. Gabriel's pail was full, and he stashed it behind a rock near the landing place, then wandered away from the water, feeling woozy from lack of sleep and an overstuffed belly.

He decided he'd wait for a while before looking for his great-grandfather's stash.

The sun was shining warmly, and Andy found a smooth rock covered with soft moss to lie on. He watched a pair of ducks swim ashore, perch on a warm rock, tuck their heads under their wings, and snooze.

"Good idea," he yawned. "Me, too."

In an instant, he was asleep.

❦❦❦

While Andy slept near the shore of Saddle Island, Jen and Kelsie explored the barn ruins. Outside was a rusty water trough overflowing with rainwater. There were four square stone walls with an opening on one side.

"This must have been the door," Kelsie said. She led Caspar over the stone sill. Inside the square, grass and small trees had grown up, covering the burnt wood.

"If we cleared the rubble out, this would make a good stable for Caspar," Jen suggested. "We just have to figure out a way to block off the door."

"And make sure the rest of the roof won't fall on his head," Kelsie added.

They got to work. Kelsie piled the big stones in one corner. Jen chucked pieces of wood and smaller stones over the wall with her good arm.

"There's not much roof left to keep Caspar dry," Kelsie said.

"He doesn't mind getting wet." Jen ginned at Caspar, who was ripping leaves off a blackberry vine that drooped over the wall. "He loves being outside."

"Good. This'll be like a big open air stall for him. Let's rig up a door so we can leave him here in the barn untied. He won't be able to jump these walls or kick his way out!"

Kelsie looked around for something large enough to block the doorway to the old foundation. She remembered the water trough. With a mighty effort she and Jen dragged it inside the door. Then they piled timbers and boards to complete the doorway.

Caspar blew happily and sucked up a mouthful of water. "Look," Jen laughed. "He approves."

"Oh, Caspar," Kelsie sighed. "I'm so glad we saved you. It was worth all the trouble."

Kelsie didn't realize their troubles were far from over!

20

Wind Rising ℗

Harefield fumed as he drove up the hill from Dark Cove. He'd forgotten all about his vow to get rid of Caspar. The horse was his, and he wanted him back. How dare those kids just waltz in and take him?

He'd show them! They'd find out they couldn't just take your horse and leave you a couple of hundred dollars. A fine horse like that. He was worth thousands, not hundreds!

He stopped his truck at the top of the hill and looked back down at the Cove. To his surprise, there was Gabriel's boat, *Suzanne*, stopped at Saddle Island. What was it doing there when Gabriel was supposed to be out fishing?

Something else twitched at Harefield's memory. Didn't that island belong to the Ridout woman?

He grunted aloud, "Could those wretched girls have taken Caspar over to the island on Gabriel's boat?" It didn't seem possible, and yet …

"It won't hurt to take a look," he said to himself. "Give me a chance to take my boat out."

He hurried back to Harefield Farms to take care of chores before he set sail in his cabin cruiser.

@ @ @

Aunt Maggie didn't worry about Andy and Kelsie being gone for lunch. Their usual routine was to be away all day—Kelsie at Harefield Farms, and Andy messing around in his motorboat, or collecting sea creatures. He'd sometimes come back for a sandwich, but not always.

It was a good day for gardening. The air was hot and still. Maybe they wouldn't get a storm after all, Maggie thought. Half the time the weather forecast was wrong.

@ @ @

Meanwhile, Jen and Kelsie were climbing the Saddle Horn. Above them rose a series of giant stone blocks, each the size of a two-story building, piled on each other.

"It's straight up," Kelsie gasped.

"Come with me." Jen gave her a sly grin. "I know a secret path."

She brushed aside spruce boughs and held them back for Kelsie. There was a narrow, zigzag track up the side of the lowest block of rock—just an animal track wide enough for one person.

Jen led the way to the top. From there it was a leap to the next tower of rock.

"We have to jump that?" Kelsie's voice shook. She didn't like heights.

"Don't look down," Jen cautioned. "It's easy." She leaped lightly across the gap, turned and held out a hand to Kelsie.

"You're part mountain goat!" Kelsie held her breath, jumped, and stood tottering beside Jen.

"We don't have mountain goats in the Maritimes," Jen laughed. "Say I'm part eagle. They have a nest up here." She pointed to a large nest in the top of a tall tree.

Up the Horn they climbed until at last Jen eased herself over the top of the peak and nestled on the rock ledge, making room for Kelsie beside her.

"I … can't," Kelsie stammered.

"Sure you can. The view is fantastic."

"No, you can keep your special place all to yourself." Kelsie hugged the pointed rock at the top of the Saddle Horn. "I'd get sick if I sat there."

"Okay." Jen swung her legs over the edge. "Maybe next time. It's great up here—you feel free as a bird."

"Birds have wings. If they fall, they can fly."

But Kelsie had to admit the view was fabulous. Looking out she could see the Atlantic coast stretching away to the north, and a vast expanse of sea to her right. If she turned her head, she could see the whole of Saddle Island, rising to a lower cliff at the south end.

"We could have horse trails all over this island," she sighed. "There'd be room to keep four, five, even ten horses, easily. Wouldn't it be fun to ride all around the shore?"

"Hmm," Jen agreed. "It's a great dream. Horses on Saddle Island. But speaking of horses, we'd better get back to Caspar."

She pointed to a bank of black clouds over the sea to the south. "It looks like the storm's coming, after all."

She stood up suddenly, making Kelsie's heart lurch, and scrambled back over the Saddle Horn. "But you can see why I love it here. It's the best place in the world."

@@@

Andy woke up with the rumbling of a powerful motor in his ears? Gabe? No, it didn't sound like Gabe's engine—too soft and purry. He rubbed his eyes and checked his watch. Two-thirty. Too early for Gabriel, anyway.

He'd been asleep a long time, Andy realized. He was stiff and sore from lying on the rock. Moss or no moss, granite was hard.

Slowly he sat up.

A large shiny white boat was edging slowly into the groove in the rock, right in front of him.

Andy rubbed his eyes again, in case he was dreaming.

No, it was no dream. The shiny white hull was coming closer. Its motor slowed to a grumbling idle.

Quickly, Andy ducked his head behind a bush. That was Harefield's cabin cruiser, the *Lord Selkirk*, coming in for a landing. What was *he* doing here?

The fog in Andy's brain suddenly cleared.

Harefield's looking for Caspar, he thought desperately. He knows we've got his horse!

Andy rolled and crept on his hands and knees across the mossy rock to the shelter of the blackberry brambles.

"I have to warn Kelsie and Jen," he whispered to himself. "Harefield's coming!"

Wriggling through the thorny vines that scratched his face and tore at his clothes, Andy reached the path at a point where he was hidden from the shore. He scrambled to his feet and raced through the brambles to the old farm.

There was Caspar—tethered outside the barn.

Where were Jen and his sister?

21

Missing Persons @

The first thing Hank Harefield noticed when he reached Saddle Island was that Gabriel's boat was gone.

"He must have left," he told himself. "Might as well take a look around and see if I can find my horse."

But it was not easy mooring the large cruiser without bashing into the rocks. There was no dock, no iron ring to tie a rope to, no flat footing to leap ashore. Harefield tossed fat foam fenders over the side to protect the *Lord Selkirk*'s shiny white hull. But with no one holding the wheel, a large wave smashed the bow straight into the rock.

Cursing, Harefield grabbed a rope and jumped over the side rail before another wave slammed the bow into the shore again. The rock was slanted and wet and he slipped half into the water trying to push her off.

Finally, he managed to tie the cruiser to a tree, scramble aboard to cut the engine and leap awkwardly to shore again.

His pants were wet, his feet soaking and his temper sizzling. When he caught those kids he'd have their hide!

Fuming, Harefield stomped off in the wrong direction—away from the farm.

He reached the other side of the island and stood panting and puffing with the effort of pushing his way through brambles and brush. Out at sea, the waves were beginning to wear white frills on their tops. The quiet day was turning stormy.

There was no sign of three kids or a white horse. Where were they? Harefield set off down the slope toward the shore, a strip of white sand revealed by the ebbing tide.

He had almost reached the beach when suddenly the ground under his feet cracked and collapsed, throwing him into a hole higher than his head. He looked up to where rotten boards had caved in under his weight. A beam of light from above showed he had fallen into a square underground room walled with dirt.

There was no way out. No ladder, no stairs, nothing to stand on. What was this? An old cellar? Some kids' fort? A booby trap? He began to shout for help.

He yelled and bellowed till his voice was hoarse and then plunked down on the dirt floor, exhausted. "No one will hear me over this wind," he howled.

<center>~~~</center>

"Andy, was this your idea of a stupid trick?" Kelsie confronted her brother. They'd heard him shouting that Harefield was coming half an hour ago, and hid in the old barn with Caspar. "Did you really see his boat? Or were you just trying to scare us?"

"Oh, sure," Andy grumbled. "And I got all scratched up running over here to warn you as part of the joke."

"Well, if you did see Horrible Harefield, where is he?" Kelsie demanded. "Why hasn't he shown up?"

Andy scrubbed his head. "How should I know?"

"It's spooky just waiting here." Jen shivered. "Let's go and see if his boat's still at the landing. The wind is rising—maybe he left."

"We'll have to take Caspar with us—otherwise Harefield might sneak up to the barn and grab him while we're gone." Kelsie snapped his lead rope to his halter. "Come on, boy."

The big horse seemed happy to be led along the path to the water. He bobbed his head and blew in Kelsie's ear.

When they reached the landing and saw the white cruiser tossing on the waves, Andy punched his sister's arm. "See, I told you."

"Ow, stop that." She punched him back. "Okay, there's his boat, but where's Harefield?"

"Looking for us, I'll bet." Jen tossed up her hands. "What are we going to do? It's almost four o'clock, Gabe will be here soon, and he won't want to wait around with the storm coming. We should get Caspar back to the barn."

"But what if Harefield finds him?" Kelsie groaned. "We can't just leave Caspar there."

"This whole thing was a stupid idea to start with," Andy sighed. "It's like all your dumb ideas. You never think things through, that's your problem."

When Andy and Kelsie weren't home at ten after five, Aunt Maggie went to the phone.

"I was wondering if my niece and nephew were at your place?" she asked Jen's mother, Chrissy. "I haven't seen them since early this morning, and they should soon be home for supper."

"I'm waiting for them, too," came the answer. "They all went out with Gabriel Peters on his boat. They were supposed to be home by now."

There was a pause. Why didn't they tell me they were going out with Gabriel, Aunt Maggie was wondering, but she knew the answer. Because she would have said no!

"Normally, I wouldn't worry," Chrissy Morrisey went on, "but I *am* a bit concerned. This storm's blowing up ..."

Aunt Maggie knew she should say something, but her throat was closed with fear. "C-call me if you hear anything," she managed to choke.

"Yes, of course, and you do the same. And if she turns up, tell Jen I want her home. I don't want her sleeping over at your place again."

"Uh—Jen slept over?" Aunt Maggie cleared her throat in surprise. "Andy and Kelsie slept out in the fish house, but I didn't see Jen ..." her voice trailed off.

"Oh! Dear!" Now Jen's mother sounded very worried. "It seems they're up to something, doesn't it? I'll see what I can find out, and we'll keep in touch."

"Yes. Of course."

Aunt Maggie hung up the phone and stood in the old-fashioned kitchen hearing the voices of another time.

It was like reliving a nightmare. A tragedy that had happened almost thirty years ago.

She ran outside, slamming the door behind her and staring out at the sea. The low clouds were greenish gray and angry. The wind whipped up whitecaps—Maggie could see the spray blowing off their tops.

"That wild girl." She clutched at her heart. "What has she done? I knew she'd find her way to some crazy mischief. It's in her—straight from her grandmother. And she's taken Andy with her. Just let them be safe!"

22

Smuggler's Stash ◎

Kelsie and Jen kept watch by the water. Harefield's white cruiser, the *Lord Selkirk*, bobbed and swayed on its rope.

"Where is Gabriel?" Kelsie groaned. "Why doesn't he come?"

Jen kept quiet. She knew if Gabriel didn't come soon, it would be hours before he could safely dock at the island again. The tide would be at its lowest in a little more than an hour, and already the muddy flats stretched far out from shore.

They could see the outline of the old causeway clearly—two rows of boulders like sharp teeth showing above the waves.

"I can see why Gabriel wouldn't want to get the *Suzanne* caught on the causeway." Kelsie shivered.

"It would rip the bottom right out of her," Jen agreed, "especially with this wind blowing from the south."

Kelsie paced the rock restlessly. "Maybe we should go to the other side of the island and see if we can see his boat."

"But if Gabe comes while we're gone," Andy mumbled, "we'll miss him. And if we're not home in time for dinner, we're gonna be in awful trouble with Aunt Maggie. She's likely wondering where we are right now."

"I don't care about Aunt Maggie!" Kelsie exploded. "You care, because she's nice to you, but I never do anything right, anyway. What's one more black mark on my record? You stay here and shout if you see the *Suzanne* coming in."

Andy squinted at her. "What if you don't hear me shout?"

"Don't worry," Jen told him, "—it's not far across the island—we'll be back soon."

They set off at a run. Kelsie insisted on taking Caspar. If Harefield came back to his boat, Andy would be no match for him.

When they reached the spot overlooking the opposite shore they saw a white sand beach with waves rolling in, but no sign of Gabriel's boat.

"If we just go a little farther, we can see around that point." Kelsie pointed to the high cliff at the south end of the island.

"All right." Jen was doubtful that they'd see anything except the empty expanse of ocean, but she tugged on Caspar's rope. "Let's go, boy."

"What's the matter?" Kelsie cried.

"He won't … budge!" Caspar had his head down, his feet planted firmly.

"Come on!" Kelsie took a step forward.

Caspar just tossed his head and pulled back.

He doesn't want you to go any farther," Jen said. "Something's wrong."

Kelsie looked down at her feet. "Look—there's some kind of hole—broken boards." She fell to her hands and knees, peering into the dark cavity. "Good boy, Caspar, we could have fallen in."

A furious voice came from the hole.

"GET ME OUT OF HERE!"

Kelsie rocked back on her heels. "Harefield!" she whispered to Jen. "How on earth did he get down there?"

Jen stared at Kelsie across the hole. She pulled back the long grass and branches.

Harefield's face glared up at them, white with fury. He'd dozed off, exhausted by shouting, but the sudden light from the hole had wakened him. "GET ME OUT!" he roared.

Just then Caspar gave another loud whinny.

"You've got my horse!" Harefield shouted. "You dug this booby trap, knowing I'd come looking for him and fall in!"

"Don't be ridiculous," Kelsie shot back. "How could we dig a hole that deep?"

"We only took Caspar because you threatened to make him into fertilizer!" Jen cried.

"And we had nothing to do with you falling in this hole." Kelsie looked down at Harefield's furious face. "We can try to get you out, if you want us to … or, we can just go away and leave you down there, which is what you deserve."

"No …" Harefield's voice was weaker. "Don't leave me."

Kelsie unsnapped Caspar's lead rope and lowered it into the hole. "Can you reach this?"

"Yes … I've got it."

"Hold on tight, and brace your legs against the side. We're going to try to haul you out."

֎ ֎ ֎

Andy was exploring the rock pools, looking for crabs. The tide was going farther and farther out, and it was getting late. Where was Gabriel? For that matter, where were Kelsie and Jen? Why did they have to go and leave him?

It started to rain. The wind swept in from the south, blowing hard enough to make the rain sting his cheeks.

There was no shelter on this stupid island, Andy thought, nowhere to get out of the storm except … he blinked the rain out of his eyes and stared at Harefield's sleek cabin cruiser. Did he dare? It would be nice and dry on that boat.

He slogged out of the shallow water, sat on a rock and put his shoes back on, all the time looking at the *Lord Selkirk* floating at the landing place. Then he stood up and walked over to where it was tied to a tree. It would just be a short leap to the deck from here …

"Get away from my boat!" Andy looked up in alarm to see Harefield's short, fat body hurtling toward him. The man's face was purple, and his clothes were black with dirt.

Kelsie and Jen trailed behind, with Caspar.

"Get away from my boat," Harefield spluttered again. "I'm going back to Dark Cove to initiate proceedings against you for horse stealing!"

As he spoke he was untying his cruiser. He leaped aboard and fired the engine. "Don't think you're going to get away with this!" he shouted over its roar. "I'll be calling the authorities the instant I land."

Andy stared at Harefield's filthy clothes. "Why is he all dirty?" he asked. "What did you do to him?"

"Nothing," Kelsie said, disgusted. "He fell down a hole. I wish we'd left him there. He isn't even grateful we pulled him out."

"What hole?" Andy stared from one to the other.

"He fell into some kind of hole over on the other side of the island." Jen threw up her arms. "He thought we'd made a trap for him—what a ridiculous idea. How could we dig a hole that big and that deep?"

"How big?" Andy insisted, in a high voice.

"We couldn't exactly measure it—we were too busy trying to yank Harefield out, and he's no featherweight," Kelsie told him. "But it looked like a small room, and it used to have boards over it, like a roof. The boards were rotten—that's why they caved in when he stepped on it."

"I know what it was!" Andy's voice rose even higher. "He fell into Roland Ridout's old smuggler's stash. Gabriel told me all about it. It was their hideout, and they hid the rum in there until they were ready to smuggle it off the island."

"Ancient history!" Kelsie said disgustedly. "Harefield's making such a fuss—as if we were teenage criminals or something. It wasn't as if we took Caspar without paying him. We gave him two hundred dollars."

"Yeah. And one hundred of it was mine. If we get in trouble over this, I want it back!"

"Come on, you two, don't fight," Jen begged. Her fine hair was plastered to her head with rain. "Look, there goes Harefield."

The cruiser had backed away from the landing and now Harefield turned the boat and opened the throttle. As the cruiser roared toward the open water, he turned to shake his fist at them.

"Look out!" Andy bellowed. "Watch the rocks."

They all shouted and waved their arms, but Harefield couldn't hear. At the last second he turned to see the rocks of the causeway dead ahead.

They heard an awful, tearing crash. The cruiser jarred to a sickening halt.

"Serves him right," Kelsie muttered.

"No!" Jen's face was stricken. "No, you don't understand. The waves will pound his boat to bits on those rocks. He has no way to get back to shore." She shuddered. "This is serious. He could drown."

"Jen, are you sure?" Kelsie asked. "Won't the tide float him off when it comes up again?"

Jen shook her head and her wet hair slapped against her cheek. "Look. He's got a hole as long as Caspar's neck in his hull."

They could all see the jagged dark rip in the smooth white hull as the waves rose and fell. "What can we do?" Kelsie cried.

"He has a big radio." Andy pointed to the antennae on top of the cabin. "He can call for help."

"It might not come in time," Jen wailed.

"Well, maybe Gabe will get here ..." Andy's eyes were scared now.

"No. Don't you understand? No boat can get through that channel at low tide in this wind. We're stuck here on the island, and he's stuck on the causeway ..." Jen's breathless voice trailed off.

23

Full Storm @

The wind rose to a screeching wail.

Here in the sheltered channel the waves slopped and heaved, but out on the causeway they thundered in, throwing huge spumes of spray into the air.

"Poor Harefield," Andy shouted, as the waves pounded the cruiser.

"It must be filling with water." Jen wiped the rain from her eyes. As she spoke, the cabin cruiser rolled at a steep angle, its deck facing toward them, its cabin smothered in water with each wave.

Kelsie stood close to Caspar, her arms around his neck. They were both drenched, but Kelsie hardly noticed the streams of water running off his mane to her shoulders. All she could think of was that this was her fault. If she hadn't had the crazy idea of bringing Caspar to Saddle Island, they wouldn't be watching Harefield's boat being battered on the rocks. If Harefield drowned, it would be her fault. Part of the Ridout curse. She *was* thoughtless and stubborn and wild, the way Aunt Maggie said. It was all true.

No wonder her family stopped living on the island, with storms like this. She hadn't understood—she hadn't bothered to find out!

She looked up at Caspar's calm face, staring out into the storm. It helped steady her raging thoughts. Maybe he came from generations of strong island horses. Maybe storms like this were nothing to him.

That gave her a sudden idea. Did she dare?

She reached out and grabbed Jen's shoulder. "Caspar and I could swim out to Harefield's boat. We could get him back to shore."

Jen spun around, rain flying from her long hair. "NO! Do you hear me, Kelsie MacKay, no! You are not going to do this—it's too dangerous."

Kelsie almost wished Jen had not put it that way. Whenever someone said NO absolutely, it made her all the more determined to do it. It felt like a switch clicked, inside. *You say no, I say yes*.

She led Caspar down to the edge of the sloping rock at the landing and started to strip off her shoes and socks.

"What do you think you're doing?" Andy shouted over the wind and waves.

"Caspar and I are going to save Harefield's miserable hide," Kelsie shouted back.

"Can't you stop her?" Andy begged Jen.

"Listen, Kel," Jen pleaded. "Just listen. I took a life-saving course. They said the first rule is don't jump in to save someone who's drowning. You could drown, too."

"Can you suggest another way?" Kelsie clambered on Caspar's back.

"No, but …"

"The water's not too rough between here and the boat. Caspar can make it. Don't worry." She hated to see the look on Andy's face—part frustrated fury, part fear—but there was no time to waste. When she looked out to Harefield's cruiser she saw it had rolled on its side and the antennae on the roof was in the water.

There was no sign of the man.

She clucked to Caspar. He trotted down the sloping rock onto the sea floor, muddy sand exposed by the out-flowing tide.

With a leap, he was in the water, and Kelsie felt its icy grip on her feet, calves and thighs. No wet suit! With a gasp, she was submerged to her waist, and only Caspar's proud, strong head was above the waves.

"Come on, Caspar!" she yelled. "Head for that boat."

Once more, the big horse seemed to know exactly where they were headed. He swam steadily into the wind.

☙ ☙ ☙

At six-thirty, Aunt Maggie's phone rang.

She picked it up as though it were too hot to touch—expecting to hear the worst.

"Miss Ridout, this is Gabriel Peters. I'm in Rossport, at the government dock. I thought I should give you and Jennifer's mom a call."

"Yes, Gabriel," Aunt Maggie choked. "Where are Kelsie and Andy?"

"I expect they're still on Saddle Island, where I left them around noon." Gabriel's voice was broken up by the storm.

"Did you say … Saddle Island?"

"Yes, Ma'am. I was supposed to pick them up at four-thirty, but I had some engine trouble and had to make for Rossport because of the storm."

"I understand," Aunt Maggie gulped. "So you think Kelsie and Andy and Jen are still …"

"Oh, I'm sure they're still on the island," Gabriel shouted over the static. "They'll be all right, just a little wet. If the wind calms, I should be able to pick them up before dark."

"Don't worry, Gabriel." Aunt Maggie's voice was stronger. "Don't take any risks. I'll call the coast guard—"

The line went dead. Aunt Maggie tried to reach the coast guard and police, but their telephone wires were down.

At last she put her head down on the kitchen table and allowed herself some tears of relief. "They're on the island. They'll be wet, but safe." Then she got up and went to the porch to reach for a raincoat. "I'd better get the news to Jen's mother, in case Gabriel can't get through," she cried, stepping out into the wind and rain.

⌀ ⌀ ⌀

At that moment Kelsie was anything but safe. The wind blew so hard that Caspar's strong legs couldn't drive them forward.

Waves smashed against them as they reached the center of the channel, away from the sheltered shore.

Kelsie wrapped her legs as tightly as she could around Caspar's belly, but she was tiring, Her hand gripping the rope was numb with cold. How long could she hold on?

Should they go back? If she turned Caspar back toward shore it would be almost easy, with the wind and waves behind them. They could be safe in no time. Maybe Jen was right and this was useless, hopeless.

She felt the stubborn will in her draining away, and with it went Caspar's will to fight on into the wind. It was just as if she'd sent him a clear message, "Turn back, while you still can."

But just then she heard a shout. She saw a white arm rise above the waves.

"Here. Here, I'm over here."

It was Harefield.

Kelsie let go of Caspar's mane and swiped the water out of her eyes. Right in front, at water level, Harefield was clinging to the side of his overturned cruiser.

She couldn't turn back. "Come on, Caspar, you're beating the wind—look where we are! Almost there! We can make it. Come on!"

It was as though she'd given the white horse a shot of courage. He surged forward, legs pumping twice as fast, snorting for air through the driving water.

Straight toward Harefield.

It would be dangerous to get too close to the sinking boat and the rocks.

"You'll have to swim," Kelsie hollered to the man. She hoped he could.

Harefield's face was white with terror, but he let go his grip on the cruiser's hull and struck out in a thrashing crawl stroke toward them.

Kelsie managed to turn Caspar out of the wind and held out her left hand to Harefield.

"Grab on," she shouted. She felt his thick, icy hand grip hers.

"Now swing your leg over his back and hang on to me," she ordered. "Grip Caspar with your legs."

"I … can't. I'm not strong enough!" Harefield howled.

"You have to! I won't be able to hold you." Already Kelsie's arm was aching. "And we didn't come all the way out here to let you drown. GET ON!"

She leaned forward, bringing Harefield's bulky body closer to Caspar's. She felt him trying to fling his leg over, once, twice, and on the third try, with Kelsie's arm nearly wrenched from its socket, she felt his bulk settle behind her and his arms encircle her waist.

"Go, Caspar!" She swung the rope to the right and signaled him to turn with her legs.

Caspar didn't need a signal. He had already swung around like a horse on a weather vane, with his tail to the wind and his head facing shore.

24

Rescue! @

In minutes, Caspar was struggling up the rocky slope.

Kelsie allowed one frozen hand to let go of his mane, the other the rope. "You can let go now, Mr. Harefield," she groaned. His weight slid away as Andy supported his slide from Caspar's back.

"Now you," Jen shouted, reaching up to help Kelsie dismount. She crumpled to her knees on the rock.

Caspar bent to sniff the tangle of soaked curls on her neck. She felt him snuffle in her ear.

"Yes, I know." She lifted her face, laughing. "You're a hero. You'd like a reward. I'm afraid it's going to have to be blackberries and rose hips for now."

@ @ @

They took shelter in the ruined barn.

Soaked and miserable, Kelsie and Jen, Andy and Harefield huddled under the slanted roof while the rain drummed down and darkness fell.

The thunder of the waves and howling of the wind was too loud to make talking possible.

It was nearly midnight when the wind died down. By that time Harefield and Kelsie had both fallen into an exhausted sleep, and Andy and Jen were both yawning so hard their jaws ached.

An hour later, almost asleep themselves, they heard the mournful blast of a boat's foghorn, and jerked awake.

"Wh-what was that?" cried Andy, struggling to his feet.

"That was a boat, come to rescue us." Jen grinned in the dark. "Let's shout!"

Soon they saw flashlight beams bobbing toward them.

It was Gabriel and his father. They had warm blankets and lights and insulated jugs of hot chocolate.

"Is Mr. Harefield here?" Gabriel asked.

"I'm here," came a weary voice.

"Thank heavens!" Gabriel's voice was hoarse with relief. "I'm afraid your boat's gone, Mr. Harefield. The tide floated her off the rocks—what was left of her."

"Doesn't matter," Harefield grunted. "The *Lord Selkirk* was insured. I can always get another boat."

He stumbled to his feet. "At least I'm alive—thanks to this girl and her horse."

He pointed to Kelsie, curled up with Caspar in one corner of the foundation.

"Did he say *my* horse?" Kelsie shot into a sitting position. "Caspar's mine?"

"I guess so," Harefield boomed. "You paid good money for

him. And without you two, I'd be at the bottom of the ocean with my boat. You're a brave kid, and he's a fine horse."

@ @ @

Kelsie didn't want to leave Caspar alone on the island overnight.

"He'll be all right," Gabriel promised her. "I've got some tools in the boat. We can make a better door and fill the water trough from the spring."

"Well, if you're sure he's safe," Kelsie yawned. "But I'm coming back tomorrow."

"I wouldn't count on that," Gabriel said doubtfully. "You put quite a scare into your Aunt Maggie."

"Aunt Maggie!" wailed Andy. "She's going to be so mad. I'll bet she never lets us out of her sight till Dad gets back."

Kelsie had an awful feeling he was right.

Gabriel put a wool blanket around her shoulders. "Come on, we'll get you on board the *Suzanne* where it's warm and dry."

Kelsie heard Caspar calling to her all the way down the path to the landing. What was she going to do about him? Was she going to lose her horse, now that he finally belonged to her?

@ @ @

Aunt Maggie sat across the table from Kelsie and Andy the next morning, her silver hair pulled back from her face, her large gray eyes fixed on their faces.

Kelsie, fidgeting on her chair, feared the worst. An explosion of anger—she'd call their father, ground them for weeks, make her give up Caspar!

Finally, after a wait that seemed forever, Aunt Maggie cleared her throat and spoke in a shaky voice.

"First, I talked to your father last night, and he is coming here in three weeks. His company gives him a paid trip every so often."

Kelsie gulped. Here it comes.

"I don't know what I'm going to tell him, about you staying here." She paused, then looked straight at Kelsie. "I thought I'd lost you both to the sea."

Kelsie nodded miserably. Andy blinked and scrubbed his head with his knuckles.

"Kelsie, you were wild and reckless—so much like your grandmother."

Kelsie choked. "I know. I saw her picture, in your album. When I was in the water I thought about how she drowned and I was afraid."

Aunt Maggie reached across the table and clasped her hand. "It's time I told you all about it. How she died. And how the word came to your father and me. It was a terrible time."

She stood up and folded her arms across her chest. Kelsie could see her aunt's fingers were white. She was holding herself hard as she spoke.

"It seems like yesterday, but it was thirty years ago," she began. "Your father and I were here in this very kitchen. The table was piled with food—all the neighbors had brought something for the potluck supper, and in the center of the table was a big cake, with 'Happy 14th Anniversary' written in pale blue icing on top. Blue—Elizabeth's favorite color. The parlor was full of friends and family, all waiting to shout 'Surprise' when Elizabeth and Michael walked in."

She paused, and looked down at Andy.

"Your father, Douglas, was thirteen, dressed up in a white shirt and dark pants, his hair slicked down. He had hair the color of yours, Andy, but longer. I remember him so clearly … he was so excited."

She paused again, and sighed. "We were waiting for their fishing boat, the *Lisa*, to dock, and the surprise party to begin. And I was happy, for once, that Elizabeth was off with Michael so I could get everything organized. Elizabeth spent too much time on that boat, when she should have been home, like a good wife, so somebody would be left to raise her son if her husband was lost at sea. That was the tradition for the wives of fishermen."

She sat back down at the table and went on. "But she never cared—loved fishing and the ocean—could never get enough."

"What happened?" Kelsie finally breathed, not wanting to hear, but not able to stand waiting any longer.

Aunt Maggie put her hand to her throat. "That day was a terrible storm, like yesterday. It was the same storm that swept away the causeway between the islands and cut them off from the mainland."

Kelsie shuddered, thinking how powerful the storm must have been to roll those enormous boulders like beach stones.

"Their boat struck a reef off the shore of Saddle Island and sank without a trace." Aunt Maggie's voice sank lower. "And we waited here in this kitchen, with the cake in the middle of the table, until word came ..." She broke off and stood again, staring at something they couldn't see.

"Your father didn't get over it for a long time. And when he did, he never wanted to talk about what happened. He moved in here—I was just twenty-five at the time—and I looked after him till he went away to work in the mines in Sydney. Then he met your mother, and didn't come home again, until now."

Kelsie got up and threw her arms around her aunt's neck. "I'm so sorry," she cried out. "I'm so sorry I frightened you like that. But I love it here, Aunt Maggie, and I love the sea and Saddle Island. It feels like home. I wish Dad would come back and live here, too."

Aunt Maggie opened her arms and hugged Kelsie back. "Do you, really?" She blinked hard. "I know I've given you a bad time."

"That's all right," sighed Kelsie. "I've been ... I can understand you'd be mad at your sister for leaving you with a thirteen-year-old boy to bring up."

"That's not why I was angry ... I think I was angry at Elizabeth because she died and left me alone. We were very close." Her face crinkled into a sad smile. "So you really love it here in Dark Cove. Then I guess you belong here. You're a Ridout, after all."

"I'm a Ridout, too." Andy leaped to his feet. "Even if I am short."

Aunt Maggie laughed a deep, hearty laugh. "You're not that small, boy. I think with some good salt air and enough bumbleberry pie you'll grow tall yet."

Her face grew serious again.

"Sit down, both of you." She sat, too, on the other side of the table. "There'll have to be some new rules, if you're going to stay."

She waggled her finger at Andy. "First, you are not to take that dory out of sight of the shore. If I catch you, I'll sell the motor and the boat."

"That's okay," Andy said sadly. "My boat sank, anyway."

"But how will we get to Saddle Island?" Kelsie broke in. "Caspar …"

"You've got to prove to me that you are responsible enough and grown up enough to go near that island again." Aunt Maggie's brows came together. "I don't want to hear about any more wild swimming on horseback."

"But Caspar …"

"And as for that horse," Aunt Maggie continued, "I understand that you have bought him from Mr. Harefield. But you'll have to keep him here in my barn. There's a perfectly good stall for a horse, for two horses, if it comes to that, and there's no reason …"

Kelsie interrupted her by grabbing her for another hug. "Do you mean it? We can keep him here?"

"Of course, you'll have to look after him yourselves. I'm not doing barn chores. It won't be easy once school starts."

25

A Horse to Share ☙

"Caspar will be your horse, too, Jen," Kelsie said with a decided shake of her head. "We'll share him, and Saddle Island, and you won't have to work at Harefield Farms anymore."

"That'll be a relief," Jen sighed. "I don't care if I ever see Hank Harefield again!"

The two of them were getting a stall ready for Caspar later that afternoon.

Outside, the storm still howled around the old barn, driving rain against the metal roof. Once it was over, they would figure out a way to get Caspar off Saddle Island, but right now there was plenty to do, putting down straw in the stall for bedding, fixing up a hay net and water bucket for him, washing the small window so plenty of light could come in.

Just then, Andy burst into the barn. "Aunt Maggie says to come. She has a surprise for us!" He gave Jen his shy grin. "You can come, too."

Kelsie, Jen and Andy hurried through the rain to the blue house. Aunt Maggie had been shut in her sun porch since the evening before.

Kelsie was worried. Was her aunt still mad at them? Would she ever get over the shock of thinking they were "lost at sea" like her sister? She knocked timidly on the sun porch door.

"Come in," her aunt's voice said over the drumming of the rain.

Kelsie slipped inside the door, with Andy and Jen close behind her.

"Watch where you step!"

Aunt Maggie pointed to the floor, where two newly hooked rugs lay. The colors were so bright they seemed to sizzle.

"When you came I decided it was time this house stopped being a museum," Aunt Maggie told Kelsie and Andy. "I've been working on some new rugs for your rooms."

Kelsie gasped. In the center of her rug was a white horse's head—a perfect portrait of Caspar. On Andy's was a boat—the green dory on a blue sea.

"Thanks, Aunt Maggie!" Andy picked up the rug and hugged it to his chest. "This is better than a picture of my boat."

"It's beautiful," Jen added.

Kelsie couldn't say anything because she wanted to cry. All that time Aunt Maggie had spent shut in her room, all the times she'd waved Kelsie impatiently away, and it was because she wanted to surprise her with this!

"We'll donate the old rugs to the historical society," Aunt Maggie said with a shake of her head.

"No!" Kelsie burst out. "I love my new rug, but I want to keep my great-grandmother's, too."

"Fine." Aunt Maggie beamed. "We'll hang it on the wall, and this one can go beside your bed."

॰॰॰

The storm blew itself out by the next morning. When Kelsie ran down to the dock she saw that the waves had washed huge driftwood logs high up on the shore. The islands seemed far away under dark gray skies. "Poor Caspar!" Kelsie mourned. "He must be wondering what's happening, and where everybody went."

And then, around the corner of Fox Island, came the *Suzanne*, tossing on the long swells left over from the storm.

Gabriel hailed her from the deck. "Were you thinking of heading to Saddle Island to see your horse?" he shouted.

Kelsie shouted back, "I'd like to, but the dory sank, and Aunt Maggie …"

I'm going past the island today," Gabriel interrupted. "Maybe your aunt would like to come, too." He leaped ashore on the Ridout dock with the rope in his hand. "Why don't you go and ask her," he suggested. "She might surprise you."

Not in a million years, Kelsie thought. Aunt Maggie would never agree to go out to Saddle Island on a fishing boat! But then she remembered how her aunt had already surprised her with the new rug.

She raced up to the house.

"Aunt Maggie?" She burst into the sun porch. "Gabriel says he'll take us out to Saddle Island to see Caspar. He says the sea is getting calmer, and he wants to know if you'll come, too."

She stopped, breathless. Aunt Maggie was gazing at her with her large gray eyes, as if she were a creature from outer space.

But I'm used to that look, Kelsie thought. She swallowed bravely. "You like picking berries—well, you should see the blackberries on Saddle Island. They're so big, and ripe, they're falling off the vines. It's a shame to waste them. If we took pails, I'll bet we could get enough to stock the freezer for the whole winter …"

Aunt Maggie stood up. "I remember the blackberries." She sighed. "They grew wild, all over the island—the best blackberries from here to Cape Breton." She straightened her back and raised her chin. "All right," she said. "Get your brother and your friend Jen, and let's go."

@ @ @

Aunt Maggie stayed in the *Suzanne*'s cabin, gripping the bulkhead, all the way to the island. Gabriel kept up a stream of talk as he steered the boat carefully into the landing. Andy was at his side watching every move.

Out on the back deck, with the wind in their faces, Kelsie and Jen couldn't hear what they said. But Aunt Maggie looked less grim-faced as Gabriel steered the boat into the channel.

"Now watch your step," he cautioned as Aunt Maggie stepped ashore. "And like I told Kelsie, meet me here by four this afternoon."

"We will," Aunt Maggie promised. "Thank you, Gabriel."

Gabriel winked and flashed a smile at Kelsie as he backed away from the rock. She felt her heart shiver. Only Gabriel, she thought, could have gotten Aunt Maggie to Saddle Island.

Her aunt dived happily into the blackberry vines with Andy.

Kelsie and Jen hurried ahead with a sack of food for Caspar. How was he doing after two nights alone in the storm? Was he all right?

For sure, she thought, he would have devoured everything fit for a horse to eat inside the ruined barn's walls—grass, small trees, weeds.

When she and Jen opened the makeshift door he was there, with his nose thrust toward Kelsie's pocket as if to say *I'm starving! What have you got for me?*

They fed him oats and apples, and then led him out of the barn ruin to find fresh grass. As Kelsie watched him grazing peacefully, Aunt Maggie and Andy arrived.

Aunt Maggie looked around and sighed. "So little left of the farm. The house used to be there ..." She pointed. "It was a beautiful house."

"The wishing spring is still here," Kelsie said.

Aunt Maggie's startled eyebrows shot up to her hairline. "H-how did you know about that?" she stammered. "The spring was our secret—Elizabeth's and mine."

"It's all right, Aunt Maggie," Kelsie hurried to say. "I just guessed about the spring. I'm not a ghost, honest. Andy and I saw an old picture of you and Elizabeth there in your album. I guessed—because that's what I would have done—made it into a wishing spring."

She watched her aunt's face relax. "Of course you would," Aunt Maggie said. "It's a funny thing how people in the same family have the same twitches and habits and odd ideas, isn't it?" Her gray eyes sparkled. "Well, then, how would you like to make a wish?"

"Yes," Andy, Jen and Kelsie all said at once.

They walked through the long grass to the spring. Standing over the clear pool, with Caspar resting his head on Kelsie's shoulder, they each wished.

"I wish Dad would come out here to the island and help me explore," Andy said.

"He will," Aunt Maggie promised. "I'll see to it. And I wish …" She paused. "No, no, I don't think I'll tell my wish. It might spoil it."

"Me, too," whispered Jen, with a shy glance at Andy.

"I'll tell mine," Kelsie cried. "I wish we could get Caspar back to Dark Cove, to his stall in the barn."

"That wish will come true, at least," her aunt laughed. "Gabriel tells me he'll take him back on the *Suzanne* today, if the weather stays calm."

"He will?" Kelsie said, astonished. "Jen told me he'd never agree to carrying a horse on his boat. She said it would be like asking him to take a pig in his Porsche."

Her aunt laughed again. "Well, he must think very highly of Caspar, or you, because he didn't bat an eye when I asked."

"You asked?" Now Kelsie was even more astonished.

"Naturally," Aunt Maggie said. "We can't leave the horse here all by himself."

As they led Caspar off toward the landing place, Kelsie turned back to look at what was left of the farm on Saddle Island. She knew she would come back and make another wish by the spring someday, a wish she wouldn't tell anyone.

She took Jen's hand. Well, maybe she'd tell Jen.

They'd have so many adventures on Saddle Island!

About the Author ම

Sharon Siamon was born in Saskatoon, Saskatchewan, in the year of the horse. Horse crazy since she was old enough to say "horse," Sharon began riding, like many of her readers, by borrowing a friend's horse. She read every horse book she could get her hands on and now writes them for young readers who share her love of horses.

Her first books, *Gallop for Gold* and *A Horse for Josie Moon*, are set in northern Ontario where Sharon, her husband, and three daughters built a log cabin. Her popular Mustang Mountain books—with a million books in print worldwide—are set in the Alberta mountain wilderness where she loves to ride. Inspiration for her new Saddle Island series came from seeing a beautiful white horse galloping along Nova Scotia's Atlantic shore. Along with horses, Sharon loves the ocean—maybe because she's a Pisces, the sign of the fish.